THE
Chicken Bus Girl
STORIES

THE
Chicken Bus Girl
STORIES

VOLUME I

NATHAN TILLOTSON

The Chicken Bus Girl Stories Volume I
Copyright © 2014 by Nathan Tillotson

All scripture quotations are taken from the New King James Version of the Bible.

Editorial service provided by Snapdragon Group[SM] Tulsa, OK, USA
Cover and design by Whisner Design Group Tulsa, OK, USA
Photography by Rebekah Elena

Library of Congress Control Number: 2014909473

Printed in the USA

I would like to dedicate this book to my wife Libby,
the original Chicken Bus Girl,
and to all those other adventurers
who love a good story.

Preface

I have always loved stories. Like a beautiful painting or a lovely song, a story speaks directly to the heart and soul. The reason for this is that God designed us to learn through words, illustration, and imagery. The Bible itself is a collection of stories that allows us to know the Creator more intimately.

Jesus almost always used stories and parables when He spoke to the multitudes. He taught figuratively in public to the masses, and spoke plainly in private with His disciples. A good story in a movie or book does that. It speaks to you figuratively on one level and plainly on another level.

I asked God to give me relatable stories that would speak to people. And He has. They come to me like a poem or song is imprinted on the mind of an artist or song writer. I tell these tales using writing paper for a canvas and a pen for a paintbrush.

The first story, *The Faith That Sees,* came to me in 2002. The story was so vivid in my mind that I did not feel a need to write it down. But after that, other stories came, so many that it dawned on me that there had to be a reason. I started typing and saving them. Still, like with my first book, *The Art of Decision,* it did not occur to me initially to put what I had received into book form.

Things took a turn in 2010 when I wrote *The Chicken Bus Girl* story. I read it to hospital staff during down-time and the response was amazing. People wanted me to read more of my stories to them on the OB ward and at the Women's Clinic.

Crew members in OR asked me to share my stories during surgery. I used my stories when teaching in churches and Bible schools and audiences were on the edge of their seats.

Libby and my co-workers encouraged me to publish a collection of my writings. Others have been asking me for several years when my short stories are coming out. Thank you for your encouragement and perseverance. The wait is finally over. *The Chicken Bus Girl Stories* have arrived!

Introduction

The Chicken Bus Girl Stories are organized alphabetically for quick reference. There are two general categories of stories depending on what you are in the mood for. The first category, *Food for the Heart,* consists of romantic tales. You will recognize those stories by the chocolate covered strawberry next to the title.

The second category, *Food for the Soul,* consists of more thought-provoking stories. You will recognize those stories by an apple next to the title.

Let me say a word about the story titles. Don't read too much into them. Just like you cannot tell a good book by its cover, you cannot tell a good story by its title.

I have subtly embedded Scripture words in the fabric of some stories. The Scripture references are found at the end of each narrative. You may or may not recognize the Scripture phrases when you are reading the story. I find this to be a new and refreshing way to read familiar verses and learn new ones.

All stories, except for personal accounts, are fictitious. *The Chicken Bus Girl Stories* cover the spectrum of life experiences and emotions. The overriding themes, however, are love, humor, and adventure, three things that make life worth living. Get ready to go on a journey of adventure food for the soul!

Contents

The Andorra Tea

Queen Sehrina sat across the table from the High Judge, sipping warm tea. She closed her eyes with pleasure as the delicious liquid coursed down her throat. "It has been long enough, Keyton. You must tell me the secret to your exquisite beverage" she told her old friend, half-jokingly. The wise, old High Judge smiled as he drank from his own cup. He was fifty years Sehrina's senior and had known her since she was born. On one level the beautiful Sehrina was his queen. On another level, he viewed her as a daughter, a feeling she reciprocated.

"Very well, your Majesty," he grinned. I suppose I will tell you the secret ingredient on this my last day as High Judge. I add a small amount of Andorra fruit juice imported from Ingomar.

The queen laughed softly. "I see. At last I know. Now that wasn't so hard, was it?" she teased. Your secret will be safe with me" she confided. "Much harder will be the task of finding your replacement," she added on a more solemn note.

The Code of the Land dictated that the ruling king or queen select the next High Judge when the preceding one stepped down or died. Her own husband, King Feydnor, died shortly after he and Sehrina were wed. Surrounded by a multitude of counselors,[1] she had wisely ruled the empire for five years At twenty five, her position and growing age required she marry and provide an heir for the empire, something she had been reluctant to do until now. Selecting the next High Judge was another big decision. The burden of command weighed on her heart at moments like this. The next High Judge would influence the affairs of the empire for years to come. The choice was hers alone.

It was common for rulers to ask the retiring High Judge's recommendations for a suitable substitute. Hence, the purpose of Queen Sehrina's visit on this occasion. This was more than protocol for Sehrina. She was seeking a trusted friend's advice. The two continued their conversation in Keyton's chamber as they approached the topic of his replacement. Sehrina eyed the stately Lord Keyton over the brim of her cup as she drank. She knew there was more to the man than met the eye.

"Keyton, do you have someone in mind for your position?"

The High Judge looked across the elegant caoba-wood table at Queen Sehrina. He rested his mug on its surface. He gazed at Sehrina's porcelain face, creamy brown hair, and stunning violet eyes. She had grown so fast, from a child to a young woman, wife, widow, and now ruler of the largest empire in the world. He both cared for and admired her greatly. He looked at her the way a loving father looks at his daughter.

"There are several men who would make a good High Judge, your Majesty. There is, however, one man who will make a *great* High Judge. I believe you will know by the end of the day who he is. I leave it to you to determine his identity."

"*That's it?* You're not going to tell me who he is?" she said incredulously.

Keyton chuckled. "I am confident you will know when you see him."

Sehrina huffed, more for dramatic effect than annoyance. "You sound like I'm choosing my next husband and not the next High Judge."

Keyton smiled. "Trust me, your Highness, you will know," he said triumphantly.

The queen looked at him skeptically. "I hope you are right for all our sakes."

"I have one small request, your Majesty. I will be presiding over my last case this morning. I would like you to stay and watch the proceedings." He pulled back the curtains across a cream textured wall, exposing a large glass window through which the kingdom of Entalah's supreme courtroom was in full view. Keyton tapped the large window with his knuckles, smiling. "Behind this one-way glass, you will be able to both observe and hear the proceedings in total privacy. My last case, a minor dispute, will start in a few moments. I beg you to remain here in my chamber and watch the proceedings."

How could Sehrina say no to her old mentor and friend? She was looking forward to hearing the case and watching the High Judge in action one last time.

"Judge Keyton, I will observe the proceedings on one condition," she said with a playful smile. Keyton raised an eyebrow.

"Yes, Your Majesty. What would that be?" he asked.

"Pour me some more of that delicious Andorra juice tea of yours." She giggled. At this the High Judge smiled brightly and poured his queen another cup.

* * * * * * *

The round theater-shaped supreme courtroom was filled to capacity with people waiting to hear the day's only case. There were balconies for rulers and special guests. The citizens of Entalah were passionate about the law, or Code of the Land as it was commonly called. They understood that adherence to the Code, given to them by the Revered One, was responsible for the empire's great strength and prosperity. Teaching in the Code was mandatory at every level of education. One day a week was dedicated to public gatherings for fellowship and discussing the principles of wisdom and morality contained in the Code. It was part of the empire's consciousness and identity.

The courtrooms of Entalah were routinely filled to capacity with people eager to hear legal cases debated according to the Code. Unlike some cultures, counselors who represented plaintiffs or defendants in legal cases were highly respected citizens in Entalah. Keyton, the High Judge, was the supreme authority in legal matters concerning the Code. Twenty-four Elder Judges served under him and helped judge the nations that made up the kingdom.[2] Everyone knew that this was the last case Keyton would be presiding over in his illustrious thirty-five-year career. It was customary for the High Judge to hear a minor case on his last day—a tradition that added to the intrigue on the day when the next High Judge was to be announced. Everyone was flush with anticipation.

"All rise!" ordered the court steward. All speaking ceased as those gathered rose to their feet. "The supreme courtroom of Entalah is now open. High Judge Keyton is officiating." Keyton walked into the courtroom from the side door of his chamber wearing a long white robe and took his seat behind a massive desk, behind which was a tinted, impenetrable glass pane. The defendant and her counselor stood below him to his left and the claimant's counselor to his right. Keyton seated himself and then opened a large book on his desk, the Code of the Land. The steward blew a large ram's horn, and its sound reverberated over all present. He then asked everyone to be seated so that the proceedings could begin. Queen Sehrina watched with fascination from her chair in Keyton's chamber. The Code of the Land would decide the day. Keyton looked at the claimant's counselor. "State your case," he said with great authority.

The claimant's counselor did not address the High Judge. Instead, he pointed an accusing finger at the defendant. All eyes followed. "This woman has been caught in the act of stealing and committing marital betrayal. According to the guidelines put forth in the Code, she must be put to death."[3] The claimant looked at the woman with condemning eyes. An ominous, palpable silence permeated the courtroom.

"Are these accusations true?" Keyton asked the woman. She kept her head down, a tear streaming down her cheek. "Yes," she said softly. A low murmur went through the crowd as those present realized that the Code did not require the woman to admit guilt, but she had done so willingly, knowing the penalty for her actions meant certain death.

From her vantage point behind the glass, Sehrina observed the woman closely. Due to the people's love for the Code, crimes like these were rare in Entalah. She couldn't help but admire the young woman's bravery for owning up to her deeds in the face of certain execution.

The defendant's counselor stood next to her. It was his duty to represent her case, as difficult as that might be. "What do you have to say in her defense, counselor?" Keyton asked.

"Her defense is the Code itself, Your Honor," he replied.

"Nonsense!" spat the claimant's counselor. "The Code clearly states the penalty for her crimes is death! There are no exceptions. She *must* die!"

Sehrina looked over at the claimant's counselor. There was not a whit of compassion in his voice. "The Code is clear," he demanded again. "She committed treason and therefore, she must die!"

A brief silence prevailed as everyone fixed their attention on the woman's counselor. Sehrina held her breath, hoping there was something he could do.

"Your Honor," he started, "the claimant's counselor is correct in stating that her actions against the Code have earned the sentence of death."[4]

Sehrina could hardly believe what she was hearing. What kind of counselor was this? He was agreeing with the defendant's accuser!

But then the counselor began to speak again. "The accuser, however, does not fully understand the greater meaning of the Code," he told the court. "It is written that the weightier matters of the Code are justice and mercy and faith.[5] You cannot have justice without mercy. The Code is a Code of justice *and* mercy."

"Mercy," whispered many in the audience.

Sehrina could not take her eyes off the defense counselor. The man's passion stirred her soul. She felt a warm sensation inside her at the sight of his black hair and dark blue eyes and solid frame. Sehrina looked at him with a combination of admiration, respect, and physical attraction. She wondered if he was married. Then shaking her head as if desperate to clear her thoughts, she said, "Get hold of yourself, Sehrina!"

The defendant's counselor concluded his remarks while looking straight at the accuser. "It is written, judgment is without mercy to the one who has shown no mercy. Mercy triumphs over judgment."[6]

The audience murmured in amazement and approval of the young counselor's defense. High Judge Keyton spoke up. "We will take half a segment recess before reaching a verdict." The ram's horn sounded. Many left the courtroom during the break period. The defendant, however, remained at her seat with her counselor by her side. Keyton stood and walked back to his chamber during the break.

* * * * * * *

"Well, what do you think?" Keyton asked Sehrina.

"About the case?" she responded.

"No, no. About him—the defendant's counselor. What do you think about *him*?" They both turned to look at him through the glass.

"He is brilliant," she admitted.

"And—" hinted Keyton.

"And dedicated, compassionate, and—"

"Handsome?" suggested Keyton.

"Why yes, he is quite handsome. But what does that have to do with anything?" she answered, sounding a bit more agitated than intended.

Keyton smiled. "Why nothing, Your Majesty. I was just wondering if you had noticed."

Sehrina eyed him suspiciously. "You are up to something, Lord Keyton, I know it!" she exclaimed. Sehrina knew her crafty friend all too well. He gave her that mischievous smile again, but this time she quickly turned the conversation to official matters.

"I believe you wanted me to see the counselor at work in consideration for the High Judge vacancy. Am I correct, Keyton?" He nodded. "I sense you approve of him highly, and I do as well. I believe he will make a fine High Judge. Let it be so."

"Yes, Your Majesty, as you wish," Keyton replied. There was a brief pause. "Let us not forget that there is also a vacancy for the king's position, Your Majesty," he reminded her, smiling playfully.

"Keyton, you have gone too far! I am fully aware of the king's vacancy. I will know who the right male is when I see him," she said, her gaze wandering to the one in the center of the courtroom.

"Why, of course Your Majesty," Keyton said while placing his hand over his chest and bowing respectfully. He made no attempt to conceal his broad grin.

* * * * * * *

The ram's horn sounded again and everyone took their seats in the courtroom. High Judge Keyton spoke up. "I have heard both sides present their cases based on the Code. The supreme courtroom of Entalah finds the defendant *guilty* of the crimes she has been accused of by the claimant's counselor." At this, the audience let out an audible gasp. Queen Sehrina put a hand over her lips. The defendant buried her head in her hands. The accuser's sinister smile told everyone that he was eagerly anticipating the condemned woman's sentencing. Meanwhile, the defense counselor remained stoic, immovable. Keyton continued.

"This court also finds the defendant deserving of *mercy* based on the Code as presented by the defense counselor. She is sentenced to two years of community improvement. It is so. Court dismissed."

Keyton closed the Code book on his desk as everyone got up from their seats to leave. The defendant gave her counselor a thankful hug, and smiling warmly, he hugged her back. Unable to do a thing about the court's decision, the accuser's eyes were bulging with rage.

While Sehrina continued to observe through the

chamber glass, Keyton signaled for the defense counselor to remain in the courtroom. Soon they were engaged in conversation near the defense table.

* * * * * * *

"You performed admirably today, Counselor Sethyo," said Lord Keyton.

"Thank you, sir. It was an honor to present my case before you on your last day in office," he replied.

Keyton smiled. "The pleasure has been all mine, I assure you," he said, looking up at the glass pane and winking at the queen. He wished he could see the look on Sehrina's face.

"I purposefully scheduled this case today so I could speak to you afterward," he admitted. The young counselor appeared confused.

"Your Honor, I do not understand. Why would you need to speak with *me*?"

"As you know, Sethyo, I am stepping down from my position as High Judge." He raised his right hand to show him something. "I have worn the High Judge's ring long enough." Sethyo looked at the High Judge's ring—the only one of its kind in the empire. It consisted of a magnificent gold band with a crest on the top. In the center was a throne, and along the perimeter were the words righteousness and justice.[7]

Sethyo was in awe of the ring and the great responsibility that came with it. He could not bear to consider what Lord Keyton might mean by these words.

"I suppose you are guessing why I am telling you all this, Counselor Sethyo," Keyton continued. "The queen, upon my recommendation, has chosen you to be the next High Judge of Entalah."

Sethyo's knees wobbled, his mind barely able to grasp what he was hearing. "Me?" he asked incredulously. Keyton smiled.

"Why me?" you ask? It is because you possess the purity of heart to be a High Judge," Keyton responded with moist eyes. "That is a rare and unique quality. Should you choose to accept it, the position is yours."

"You and her highness the queen have placed great trust in me," Sethyo said humbly, looking down.

Keyton looked toward the window. "The queen trusts my judgment," he said, winking again with a hint of a smile. Sehrina rolled her eyes on the other side of the glass.

Sethyo said nothing for a few moments as he thought about how drastically the position of High Judge would change his life. "I accept the responsibility of High Judge," he said finally. "Though it will take some getting used to being addressed as such."

"Good! Tomorrow it will be made official. The queen will take the ring off my finger and place it on yours. There's still some business we need to take care, though. Come with me."

* * * * * * *

Sethyo followed Keyton into the High Judge's chamber. A woman with her back to them was wearing a beautiful soft orange Carrisian silk dress. A diamond-studded holder accented cascades of light brown hair that flowed down to her slim waist. A creamy white neckline was graced by a simple but elegant silver choker studded with black jade stones. Her alidian perfume filled his nostrils, heightening his senses. He was well past allured at this point, though he had not yet seen her face. In a word, the woman was captivating.

"There is someone here to see you, Your Majesty." As

Sehrina turned to face the two of them. her mesmerizing violet eyes met Sethyo's. He stopped instantly, as if a hand had reached into his soul and clutched his heart. Keyton nudged him lightly on the shoulder, and Sethyo abruptly came to himself and bowed, closing his eyes.

After a brief pause, the queen spoke. "You may rise," she said. Her exquisite voice was the perfect match for her beauty, elegance, and inner strength.

Keyton smiled ever so slightly at Sethyo. "Tomorrow you will be presented before the people as High Judge. As such, you must always serve our people with compassion."

Sethyo looked respectfully at Queen Sehrina. "Yes, Your Majesty! I will strive to do so always."

The queen's cordial smile made him feel warm all over. Sethyo was having difficulty suppressing the effect Sehrina was having on him. He had no idea that Sehrina was experiencing some of the same challenges. She might be a queen but she was still a woman. Keyton was enjoying himself immensely. He finally decided to come to their rescue.

"Would you like something to drink, Sethyo?" he said casually, more a statement than a question. He pulled an elegant crystal flask from a transparent warmer and offered Sethyo a cup of tea. The counselor drank Keyton's secret formula gratefully as Sehrina observed him.

"Would you like to guess what is in this drink?" he asked Sethyo.

"If I am not mistaken, I taste a bit of Andorra juice, a rare fruit that grows only in Ingomar, Lord Keyton." He took another sip of the delightful beverage

Sehrina was impressed, and Keyton was beaming with approval as he addressed the queen. "Your Majesty, there are some things the three of us should discuss this evening before tomorrow's ceremony."

"Very well," Sehrina replied. "We will discuss these issues over dinner at the palace."

"As you wish, Your Majesty," Keyton replied. "Sethyo, your wife may join us for dinner tonight. I would very much like to meet her."

Sehrina eyed Keyton suspiciously. *What is he up to now?* she wondered.

"I am single, Lord Keyton. I have no wife."

"No wife?" Keyton answered with feigned surprise. He placed a paternal arm around the counselor's shoulder. "I see. Just come as you are then," he responded, smiling inconspicuously as he escorted Sethyo out of his chamber.

"Until tonight, Your Majesty," Keyton concluded, meeting Sehrina's eyes and cheerfully waving a hand as they left.

Lord Keyton has been quite impossible today, Sehrina thought as she shook her head, smiling at her incorrigible friend. Even so, she could not deny that this new counselor, Sethyo, was the first person to elicit such feelings in her since Feydnor. He was going to be the new High Judge, and they would be seeing each other on a regular basis. The very idea caused her to tingle on the inside. She felt both excited and unnerved at the prospect. *What is happening to me?* she wondered. *Am I losing my mind, losing control of my senses, or experiencing feeling for someone again? Perhaps all three!* She couldn't tell. "Revered One, help me!" she whispered.

The thought of being married to someone like Sethyo was not totally displeasing. She recalled his intelligence, pleasing personality, and good looks, not necessarily in that order. Had the ingenious Lord Keyton found her a High Judge *and* a husband at the same time? If anyone could achieve such a feat, it would be him. The prospect amused Queen Sehrina.

She recalled an obscure phrase from a primitive planet named Earth that seemed to fit the situation. Two for the price of one. *I think I like the idea,* she thought, smiling and savoring another sip of Lord Keyton's Andorra tea.

[1]Proverbs 11:14; 24:6

[2]Revelation 4:4

[3]John 8:3–5

[4]Romans 6:23

[5]Mathew 23:23

[6]James 2:13

[7]Psalm 89:14

The Bold Squirrel

Have you ever wondered why God made squirrels? I have. I've also wondered why He wired them the way He did. If I didn't know better, I would think most squirrels' wires were not connected at all. They never seem to be able to make up their minds! I'm sure you have your own experience with these ditsy rodents. Let me share one of mine.

Our family lived on-post at Fort Sill, Oklahoma, my last year on active duty. I had three routes to choose from to go to work at the hospital in the mornings. The most pleasant and scenic route was through the neighborhood in front of the Officer's Club. It was a peaceful and quiet area with many historic homes. There were huge trees everywhere, with a couple of open fields for recreation and sidewalks for joggers. A golf course and small wildlife area were located next to the club. In front of the club, two rows of large oaks lined both sides of the street like sentinels. The speed limit on this small stretch was fifteen miles per hour. The tranquil drive was a reprieve from the rigors of a busy OB/GYN physician. Only a squirrel could ruin it for me.

As I approached the club on my way to work one morning, the little furry guys were everywhere, chasing one another, going up and down trees. They were doing everything but watching for cars. I slowed down to fifteen miles per hour, initially amused by the rodents' playful, care-free lives. Then a particular squirrel caught my eye. It was about thirty yards ahead of me, cutting a path back and forth across the street. Even though my car was coming closer and closer, the little fur ball was oblivious to my presence or the imminent danger of being run over.

Back and forth he went, left to right, right to left, time after time. *Surely he is going to notice me before I get to him*, I thought. No such luck. *Will you please make up your mind!* I remember thinking. I slowed down to a snail's pace, almost stopping completely. Only then did he notice me, darting across the road to my left and running up a nearby oak beside the sidewalk. I looked over at him in exasperation. He was hanging from the side of the oak tree, staring at me. *"You are such a squirrel!"* I said to him, as if he could hear or understand me. Needless to say, my opinion of squirrels dropped temporarily after that incident. I say temporarily because the Lord reminded me of another encounter with one of His furry little creatures. That incident took place seven years earlier when I was stationed at Fort Leonard Wood, nestled in the Missouri Ozarks.

Our military home had a huge yard that backed up to the woods. Our three girls were ages five to nine at the time. There was a groundhog named Chucky who lived near our tree line. He had a steady supply of apples tossed near his hole in the ground all year long. We had a suet feeder that attracted woodpeckers daily. We also installed a very popular bird bath for our avian friends. Deer could be seen traveling through the woods behind the house from time to time as well. I also planted a cherry tree in our back yard. We never harvested any cherries ripe enough to eat, but the blue jays certainly did. Our home in Fort Leonard Wood was the girls' favorite during our twelve years on active duty, thanks to our backyard animal sanctuary.

The center of activity in our yard was a large, three-cylinder bird feeder. It was ten feet away from the patio, hanging from a large tree branch. I filled the three large transparent tubes with sunflower seeds, and we were open for business. We had forty to fifty birds around our feeder in no time. The girls were absolutely delighted. We watched them from inside the house through the back window so as not to scare them. It was a little bit of heaven until the squirrels started showing up. That's when I experienced the epic battle waged by so many homeowners before me—*man versus squirrel!*

Round One began with me hanging the feeder four feet above the ground and twelve feet away from the tree trunk, according to instructions. This made it impossible for the squirrels to reach the feeder by jumping from below or from the tree itself. I was pretty pleased with myself when the squirrels' attempts at reaching the prize in this manner proved unsuccessful. But my victory was short-lived. I woke up one morning a few days later to find the bird feeder lying on the ground. The heavy-duty nylon string I used to hang the feeder had been chewed and cut by *you know who.*

Round Two began with me hanging the feeder in the same location, this time with heavy-duty metal wire. Again, I was pleased with my ingenuity, knowing the birds would be able to eat in peace, while the squirrels would have to settle for the scraps that fell from the table. I thought this was a reasonable arrangement, but the furry fellows didn't think so. They tried reaching the bottom of the feeder from the ground to no avail. They lunged themselves from the tree trunk to the feeder, falling inches short. I hung the feeder according to specifications, just beyond their reach. I watched with satisfaction, perhaps too much, as they missed their target time and time again. They tried to chew the wire without success. I leaned back on my couch in the den and enjoyed the wildlife spectacle again and again.

It wasn't long, however, before I noticed the squirrels were up to a new trick. When I say squirrels, I mean *many* squirrels. There were anywhere from six to fifteen of them in our yard at any given moment. We had a squirrel infestation, if that is possible. All those squirrels had one mission in life: to get to the bird feeder. *My* bird feeder. You won't believe what they did next!

Once the squirrels realized they could not reach the feeder from the ground, tree trunk, or by chewing the line, they moved on to their Plan B. Albeit with difficulty, they began climbing down the eight feet of wire from the large tree branch to the top of the feeder! Once they reached the top of the feeder, they inched their way to the edge, hanging onto the hook at the center of the feeder with their hind toes. They then would let themselves freefall to the bottom of the feeder below, like something out of an Indiana Jones movie. The birds would all scatter while Indi would hike his hind leg on to the feeder tray and then proceed to gorge himself with sunflower seeds. I watched this drama unfold with a combination of shock, amazement, disbelief, respect, and annoyance. The bell rang, marking the end of Round Two.

Round Three began by me installing a large plastic baffle over the roof of the bird feeder. The squirrels would climb down the wire but could not reach the bottom of the feeder when they let themselves go from the edge of the baffle. About one in a hundred attempts was rewarded with a successful grasp of the bottom of the feeder with one hand by a totally committed and relentless rodent. That was a percentage I could live with. It was thoroughly entertaining as well. At last, I thought to myself, my bird feeder is as squirrel proof as humanly possible. I thought I had won the match in Round Three. Little did I know Round Three wasn't over yet. You see, nobody ever told the squirrel the match had ended.

Winters in Missouri can be pretty cold, below freezing at times. One chilly winter morning, I stepped out the back door with a large tub of bird seed for the bird feeder. This would help our little bird friends make it through hard times. I set the large tub on the ground while I unhooked the three-tube feeder from the wire. I removed the lid from the tub and, using a plastic cup, I started filling the tubes with sunflower seeds. Just then, something remarkable happened that I will never forget. A single squirrel, which had been observing me, ran across the yard from the tree line and stopped two feet in front of me. I towered over him, and yet he looked up at me as if asking politely for some bird seeds.

I couldn't believe what I was witnessing! I stood there for several seconds watching him with admiration. I was over two hundred times his size! And still, he just waited patiently. I bent down and scooped a cup of sunflower seeds from the tub and poured it on the ground in front of him, and then stood back to see what he would do. The cold, hungry, skinny little squirrel proceeded to fill his cheeks with as much bird seed as possible as quickly as possible. Once his mouth was full, he darted back to the woods. *That* was the end of Round Three.

The Lord reminded me of the incident with the bold squirrel after almost running over the ditsy one by the Officer's Club. Sometimes we go back and forth, not knowing what to do about a situation. If we would just approach God with the boldness of a squirrel, we might get our prayers answered sooner.[1]

---

[1] Hebrews 4:16

The Call

Jimmy did not know where he was or how he got there. He looked around. The place was beautiful. He had never seen anything this grand before. He turned slowly, trying to take it all in. He found himself inside an enormous building with a gold ceiling hundreds of feet above him. There were gigantic round columns everywhere. The marble pillars were white and embedded with precious stones of every color imaginable. No two structures were alike. They were as big as the redwood trees Jimmy had seen on a camping trip once. The walls were of the same white marble. This marble had plumes of blue throughout, like a break in the clouds. These clouds moved, however. He could not stop staring at the walls. Nobody back home was going to believe *this*.

Jimmy eventually looked down. The perimeter of the enormous hall was lined with the most beautiful wood floors he had ever seen. There were many different designs and colors to the floor. "Who could possibly live here?" he asked himself. He would soon find out.

The little boy could hear two voices carrying on a conversation. He could not see them right away, because of one of the giant pillars between him and the speakers. Cautiously he pulled up close behind the pillar and started making his way around it hoping to catch a glimpse of who was doing the talking. Would he be in trouble for being here? He looked in the direction of the conversation in the center of the great hall.

The floor in the center of the great room was made of blue crystal.[1] In the middle of the hall there were three gigantic thrones. In the middle throne there was a magnificent king with a glistening white robe, white hair, and beard. His faced seemed to glow. Jimmy could not make out his features well, but he gave the impression of warmth and great power. This king was seated on his throne and was talking to another king who was standing to his right.[2] The second king appeared younger, but his robe was equally beautiful. This king appeared strong, fearless, and peaceful. If the two kings knew Jimmy was behind one of the great pillars, they did not say anything about it—not yet. Jimmy's heart was racing as he listened intently to their conversation.

"We need someone to lead our people against the forces of evil," said the older king.

"The prince of shadows is cunning indeed, father. He destroys the lives of everyone who falls under his control.[3] All we need are vessels who will give their lives for the Kingdom of Light to defeat this enemy."

The father continued with his thoughts. "Yes, my son, but whom shall I send, and who will go for us?"

"Here I am! Send me," whispered Jimmy. *There's no way they can hear me*, he thought. But he was wrong!

"Who said that?" exclaimed the great king on the center throne. The two rulers looked in the direction of the pillar where Jimmy was hiding. "Come now, lad, let us have a look at you."

Jimmy did as he was told and stepped into the open. *Woe is me! I've been discovered. Now I'm doomed!* thought Jimmy.[4]

The father king and his son looked at the boy and then at each other and smiled. The younger king invited Jimmy to come and join him and his father. "Hello, Jimmy, how are you?" the father king said.

"You know my name?" Jimmy stammered in amazement.

"Yes, of course we know your name," the younger king said. "Your parents have done a good job raising you. Do you like this place?"

"Oh, yes sir. This place is beautiful," Jimmy answered. "May I ask who you are?"

"I AM the Judge King. That is who I AM," replied the ancient one.[5]

"And I AM the Warrior King. That is who I AM," replied his son.[6]

The boy gazed over to the empty throne on the Judge King's left. "Who does that throne belong to?" he asked.

"That throne belongs to the Helper King. He is currently doing just that, helping our people against the prince of the darkness.[7] My son, the Warrior King, will be joining him very soon. We will soon be victors in this war between good and evil."

Jimmy could sense the goodness and warmth in these two great kings. He was drawn to them. "Can I sit on your lap?" he asked the Judge King before he could stop himself. The ancient king laughed heartily and with delight beckoned him to climb aboard. As Jimmy drew near, the Judge King reached down and picked Jimmy up with his massively powerful arms and placed him on his lap. Jimmy instinctively rested his head on the ancient king's bosom. The ancient King wrapped his arms around the boy while the Warrior King caressed his hair. Jimmy felt an overwhelming flood of love and peace come over him. Tears began to run down his face. The ancient king wiped the tears from Jimmy's face with one hand.[8] He then gently deposited them in a diamond bottle held in his other hand.[9]

"No tears fall to the ground here, Son," he said. Jimmy

eventually let himself down from the Judge King's lap.

"You are very brave, Jimmy. You must be trained, however, in order to be an effective soldier in the Army of Light," the Warrior King explained. "The training ground where you will be equipped is called the Pillar of Truth.[10] This white tower, built with living stones, spirals upward toward heaven.[11] There you will receive your training from five different instructors. How far you excel in your training is up to you.[12]

"Your first instructor is called 'the builder.' He starts beachheads on enemy shores. He leads the first wave of assault into enemy territory. Your second instructor is called 'the messenger.' He is a special envoy from headquarters. He relays special instructions and encouragement from the Judge King. Your third instructor is called 'the recruiter.' He has a commanding voice. He recruits new soldiers behind enemy lines from the prince of shadows, oppressive regime. Your fourth instructor is called 'the overseer.' He is the local base commander. He is the commander of the local training center. Your fifth instructor is called 'the counselor.' He provides instruction on the finer points of warfare. He helps complete your training."

Young Jimmy looked into the Warrior King's eyes. He could feel the warmth in his smile. "Are you sure you are ready to do this, Jimmy? Have you counted the cost?"[13]

"I am ready, sir. I'll do my best."

The Warrior King was pleased.[14] "I know you will, Jimmy. I believe in you."

Jimmy woke up, his bedroom surroundings slowly coming into focus. He was trying to take in everything he had experienced. Was it just a dream? Was it real? He lay flat in bed staring up at the ceiling, definitely not made of gold. He looked over to the night table on his right. The family picture confirmed he was back home. *We make quite a team*, he thought about his family.

"Good morning, honey," his mom said as she walked into his room and gave him a big hug. "Let me take a look at you."

Just a coincidence, he thought to himself.

"It's time to get dressed and ready for church, dear. See you downstairs in a bit." With that she left him to get prepared. Jimmy didn't know what to think. Should he share his dream with his parents or just keep it to himself for now?

Jimmy could not remember the praise and worship that morning. His mind was still in a daze. *I wonder what the overseer, I mean pastor, will be speaking on today*, thought Jimmy.

The man of God stood behind the pulpit and opened his Bible to the Old Testament. Then he began to read: "'In the year that King Uzziah died, I saw the Lord sitting on a throne, high and lifted up, and the train of his robe filled the temple,'" the pastor began.[15]

Jimmy could not believe what he was hearing. *Is this another dream?* he wondered.

The pastor continued the sermon. "'The posts of the door were shaken by the voice of him who cried out, and the house was filled with smoke. So I said—'"

"'Woe is me, for I am undone!'" whispered Jimmy, completing the sentence.[16] His mother looked down at him curiously.

The pastor continued the sermon. "'Also I heard the voice of the Lord, saying: "Whom shall I send, and who will go for Us?"'"

"'Here I am! Send me,'" whispered Jimmy, a tear in his eye and a smile on his face.[17]

[1] Revelation 4:6

[2] Acts 7:55–56

[3] John 10:10

[4] Isaiah 6:4–5, 8

[5] Exodus 3:14

[6] John 8:58

[7] John 15:26

[8] Revelation 21:4

[9] Psalm 56:8

[10] 1 Timothy 3:15

[11] 1 Peter 2:5

[12] Ephesians 4:11–12

[13] Luke 14:27–28

[14] Hebrews 11:6

[15] Isaiah 6:1

[16] Isaiah 6:4–5

[17] Isaiah 6:8

The Chicken Bus Girl

You know the relationship is serious when a girl gets a passport and will go with you to a banana republic where she does not speak a word of *Local*. I'm not talking ritzy hotels, massive buffets, pristine beaches, and fresh coconut milk at the five-star resort. No, my friend. Relaxing, yes. Comfortable, yes. Romantic, perhaps. But that would do nothing to test our commitment to one another. I'm talking about something far better. I'm talking about a *real* banana republic adventure! I am talking about Snow White from the South swept away to a far-off land by a rugged American Latino. That's how the fairy tale should read. I'll give you a moment to catch your breath and wipe the tear from the corner of your eye. Let me know when you are ready for me to continue.

It all began innocently enough. I was a pre-med college junior going back to Guatemala for a couple of weeks during summer vacation to visit family and friends. Elizabeth was working on her graduate degree from Texas A&M. We had been dating for a little over a year, and she had heard many of my stories about growing up in Central America. She knew about the tropical food, friendly people, festive music, great weather, and inexpensive merchandise. All I did was extend an invitation for her to come with me. How could she resist?

We flew directly from Houston into Guatemala City. There we were greeted by the daunting presence of a volcano visible from the terminal. All this was new for Elizabeth. She took everything in while following my lead. We exchanged our green dollars for red, purple, blue, and orange Quetzals. I translated for her as we went through immigration and customs, police with pistols and soldiers with semi-automatics everywhere. We exited the terminal surrounded by a large mass of humanity. Cab drivers were competing for our business, so I negotiated a price with our driver and off we went. If you're not a Christian before you get into one of these taxis, you will be by the time you get out. Many people have been known to bargain with God for their lives during one of these terrifying rides. It was, for Elizabeth, the most memorable part of the trip.

We wove in and out of traffic at NASCAR speed, barely missing a crash every few minutes. There is barely time to recover from one close call before bracing for another. Getting behind the wheel in Guatemala City is not for the faint of heart. Being a pedestrian takes real guts too. Driving a moped or motorcycle is sheer insanity, but you see them everywhere, darting through traffic with laser-guided precision. In Latin America, the drivers have the right of way. It's one big game of chicken, which brings me to the subject of Pollo Campero.

Pollo Campero is Spanish for country chicken. And in this country, Pollo Campero is big business, the fast food giant of Central America. There simply is no competition. Their spicy fried poultry is out of this world. They have franchises everywhere—almost always packed. There's just nothing like having Pollo Campero in Guatemala City with your sweetheart.

Elizabeth and I left early the next morning on a charter bus. Picking up pastries at the bakery around the corner from the terminal was an absolute must. We started our four-hour trip from Guatemala City nestled in the mountains to the northern coastland. The scenic ride and tropical music was great fun.

We arrived at our drop-off point around 11:00 a.m. From there, we would go ten miles by chicken bus on a dirt road through hills and jungle to Lake Izabal and a town called Mariscos. At Mariscos we would climb aboard a passenger boat for a two-hour ride to my hometown of El Estor.

In Latin America the word *passenger* means commerce. At the drop-off point, there was a small restaurant and snack shop where travelers could get something to eat and an inn off the highway that existed for the sole purpose of providing a night's stay for souls who missed the chicken bus to Lake Izabal and had to wait until tomorrow. You could sometimes pay a vehicle going to Mariscos if you didn't make the bus, but that was pretty much hit or miss. At Mariscos the bus dropped off passengers at the lake shore where the boat for El Estor was waiting.

Back at the highway intersection, we had a one-hour wait before we got on our bus. People began taking their seats as noon approached. The ladies usually got in first so they could have a seat and not have to ride standing. Three to a seat was expected, no matter what. All the windows were rolled down to let in as much fresh air as possible. Occasionally the ladies were accompanied by a chicken that evaded Pollo Campero but had an uncertain fate at their destination. The bus was always packed, but there was always enough room to fit everyone, somehow.

Over the years, I learned to wait until the last minute to get on the chicken bus. It got really hot in there sometimes. Growing up, I noticed people occasionally rode on top of the bus to and from Mariscos. I used to think they were crazy, until I was old enough to try it myself. The bus had a large metal rack for baskets and luggage. You could ride on the bus rack safely with the air blowing across your face during the trip. I was hooked after the first try and always rode up top after that.

Elizabeth and I had a bite to eat at the *restaurante,* and then it was time to board. I did not want us to ride packed like sardines, so we climbed up the ladder at the back of the bus. We did this despite the fact that women never ride on top of a bus in Guatemala. It's considered culturally unacceptable. A lady is simply not allowed to be put at risk like that. The bus driver's assistant saw us climbing on the rack and began to gesture frantically while shouting in Spanish, "You cannot do that! Women are not allowed on top of the bus!" To this I calmly replied, "She is an American." Somehow, that made all the difference. "Ah, an American!" he said, waving us on without another thought.

The bus fired up its engine and we began our ascent into the jungle. The thirty-minute ride took us through beautiful tropical hills. All five of us riding on the luggage rack were having a blast. I could tell Elizabeth was enjoying the adventure as well. She smiled at me as we cut through the winding hills, Lake Izabal visible in the distance as we eventually made our descent.

I looked across at her and made a startling realization. In the middle of that rain forest on a cool, breezy day, on top of a chicken bus, I had found my soul mate. This girl would go anywhere with me in the name of love. I knew what every great hero knows. You need a woman like that by your side. Every Tarzan needs a Jane. Every Robin Hood needs a Maid Marian. Every Superman needs a Lois Lane. The list goes on and on.

My heart was swelling with emotion as I thought about the possibilities. I would have proposed to her in that Kodak moment, if not for the other three people on top of the bus hanging on for dear life. A missed opportunity, I know you're thinking, but there would be others. I snatched her up before anyone else could see what I saw in her. Snow White from the South ended up marrying that rugged American Latino.

There would be many more adventures, some through valleys and many on mountain tops, but one thing remained constant. With God and this girl by my side, I was invincible. Who says they only live happily ever after in fairy tales? They haven't read this story. They haven't met my chicken bus girl.

Who can find a virtuous wife? For her worth is far above rubies.
Proverbs 31:10

The Cowboy Church

The 2012 Lexus ISF glided over the black Texas country road like a stealth bomber. Its ultrasonic blue-mica color and tinted sun roof looked out of place for this tranquil eastern corner of the Lone Star state. The 416 horsepower V-8 purred like a kitten at the maximum speed limit as it whizzed past country homes and ranches. A dairy cow chewing a mouthful of grass raised its head to observe the speeding passerby. The sophisticated LCD display, voice-controlled navigation system waited for the next command from its driver. He glanced down at the screen for a second. "Destination assist," he chuckled. "I sure could use some of that," he said, glancing at his rearview mirror. "Where now, Lord?" There was no reply. Jack was left to his own thoughts.

You could not have written a better script for Jack Hamilton's life until now, a pioneer and leader in the faith movement worldwide. He pastored a mega-church in Los Angeles that was more than fifty-thousand members strong, with its own Christian, Bible, and missions schools. He had a national and international television and radio ministry. He was the author of twenty-three Christian books, a board member of the largest Christian university in the country, and a highly sought-after speaker. Jack Hamilton was one of the most influential Christian leaders on the planet. He seemingly had everything going for him, until several months ago, when his world was turned upside down.

That's when he discovered his wife had been cheating on him for the last eighteen months. She divorced Jack and ran off with the man, a member of the congregation, as soon as the papers were finalized. She got half of everything in the settlement. Her last words to him were, "I don't want to be a pastor's wife anymore."

When the story hit the news, there was a huge sweep of support for Jack from his congregation and around the country. He continued ministering from the pulpit despite what a member of his own flock had done to him. Attendance at Living Valley Church swelled as people were drawn to Pastor Jack and his ordeal. He tried as best he could to continue to minister from the podium. He could go no further, however. Four weeks after the divorce, Jack informed the church board and congregation that he was taking a three-month administrative leave of absence. Dennis North, the associate pastor, was temporarily placed in charge until Jack's return. Jack rescheduled all speaking engagements for the next thirty days. He needed some time to get alone with God and clear his head. That's how he found himself in east Texas driving in the middle of *nowhere*. "Nowhere?" came the reply from a voice inside. Jack recognized God was speaking to him.

"Forgive me, Lord. I am just not sure what I am supposed to do next and where I am going. I know You are with me and are leading me."

Trust Me, My son. Jack could sense warmth covering him that comforted him greatly.

Just then, Jack's Lexus started groaning loudly and slowed down markedly. His car's speed dropped to thirty-five miles per hour. "What's going on?" Jack asked himself as he looked at the control screen. He stepped on the gas pedal with no response from the engine. He continued down the two-lane road for several minutes before seeing a sign indicating the next town: CARLISLE, POPULATION 5,429. Jack was relieved to make it safely to a town, albeit a small one. The first traffic light in Carlisle had a Texaco gas station at the corner. Jack pulled into its parking lot and went inside the store to talk to the manager.

The gas station owner was a tall, pleasant white-haired man with blue eyes and a strong Southern accent. "Sounds like your transmission is going out, my friend," he told Jack confidently.

"I thought that might be it," Jack replied, scratching his head. "Do you know of someone in town who can fix my car?"

"Nobody in Carlisle can fix a Lexus transmission. You'd have to go to Ashton about twelve miles away. They have a Lexus dealership. Bobby, the owner, is a friend of mine. If you want, I have a nephew in town who can tow your car out there. He can get you a loaner vehicle while they work on your transmission."

Jack was so thankful. God always provided. "I appreciate your help Mr.—"

"Tommy Smith at your service," the man replied with a smile. "You'll be needing a place to stay in Carlisle until they fix your Lexus. My wife, Sally, is the manager of a nice hotel just down the street. It's called the Lamp Post. I'd be glad to give her a call and let her know you will be needing a place to stay after you get back from Ashton this afternoon, if you'd like. You can join us for dinner at our house after you get checked into your room. We're havin' barbeque ribs. Gotta say, Sally makes the best ribs around."

Jack was amazed by the hospitality Tommy had offered to a perfect stranger. He couldn't help thinking that Ashton might have nicer accommodations, but how could he say no to such Southern kindness?

As if reading his thoughts, Mr. Smith spoke up. "I'm sure you would enjoy your stay here. The hotel has everything you could need and Sally is a great cook. We'd show you around if you like, make sure you have a memorable time.

"Thanks, Mr. Smith," Jack answered. "You are very kind. I happily accept your invitation!"

Mr. Smith smiled. "So it's settled. We will see you at the house at 7:00 p.m. after you get checked in at the Lamp Post."

* * * * * * *

The Smiths lived on a seven-hundred-acre ranch on the outskirts of Carlisle. Tommy was right about his wife's ribs. They were the best he'd ever tasted.

"Those were award-winning baby-back ribs, you just had," Tommy informed Jack. Just then, Sally tried to pile more on his plate, but Jack assured her that he couldn't possibly eat another bite. He had barely managed to finish off the baked beans, cornbread, and blackberry cobbler that came with the ribs.

Jack looked over at Tommy in genuine amazement. "How do you stay so lean married to such a wonderful cook?" he asked. Sally laughed.

"Why, that's simple," Tommy responded with a twinkle in his eyes. "My secret is in this here hollow leg of mine." With that, he pointed to his right lower extremity underneath his denim jeans.

"As you can see, Jack, my husband is a big kidder. You should hear some of his fishing stories. He has a very vivid imagination," Sally said with a broad smile.

Tommy continued undeterred. "What do you mean? Those stories are all true!"

Jack found the back-and forth exchange between Tommy

and Sally enjoyable. It was obvious they genuinely loved each other. *A very blessed couple,* he thought.

Suddenly, Tommy changed the subject. "Bobby at the Lexus dealership tells me it's going to be a week before they can get the parts they need and fix your transmission. I hope you weren't in a real big hurry."

Jack wasn't happy about the prospect of a delay, but he had to admit he was having a good time. Maybe it wasn't a big deal. He shared with the Smiths that he was a California preacher on his way to Tennessee to visit his sister. "A one-week delay isn't a big problem," he informed Tommy and Sally.

Mr. Smith was delighted to hear that Jack was a preacher. "You'll have to join us for church service tomorrow. Sunday morning service starts at 10:00 a.m. We'd be happy to pick you up at the hotel. No need to dress up—just come as you are. We'll see you about 9:45."

"Thank you for the invitation," Jack replied. He couldn't help but think it would be nice to be an inconspicuous visitor at a church service. That hadn't happened for years. This little corner of east Texas seemed like another world compared to the hustle and bustle of a big-city mega-church.

****

The Smiths SUV drove five miles north of town along the two-lane highway. Jack listened to country gospel as he relaxed in the back seat and took in the scenery. For fifteen minutes, they drove over rolling hills covered with blue bonnets and other wildflowers. Then he felt the vehicle slow down and then pull into the asphalt parking lot of a huge, modern church building. Jack's eyes were fixed on a large metal sculpture at the front of the building. It was a glossy black statue of a cowboy on one knee, bowing before a cross, hat in his hand and horse by his side. The huge sign on the front of the building read COWBOY CHURCH.

Vehicles, mostly pick-ups and SUVs, poured into the parking lot like a metallic herd. Tommy and Sally waved at friends as they walked toward the sanctuary building. Tommy was wearing a long-sleeve checkered shirt, straight leg jeans' and alligator boots, with a rancher's belt and buckle to match. Sally looked elegant in her long, flowing Sunday dress. Jack walked beside them wearing a polo shirt, jeans, and walking shoes. They were greeted at the door by Billy, a friend of the Smiths.

Twenty minutes before the service started wasn't enough time to visit with all Tommy and Sally's friends. Bobby, the Lexus dealership owner, was there and introduced his wife Amanda' and their two kids. Jack had been in Carlisle for less than twenty-four hours and already he felt right at home. The praise and worship team took the stage, signaling that the service was about to begin. Tommy and Sally took a seat in the third row with Jack.

Early in the service, the pastor asked visitors to raise a hand. Jack obliged and was greeted with applause from the audience and a welcome packet from one of the ushers. The message was on trusting God to direct your paths, something Jack received with watery eyes. Several people shook his hand at the end of the service, urging him to come back.

After the service, Tommy and Sally motioned Jack to follow them. There were some people they wanted to introduce him to. There was a group of people conversing in the altar area between the front row and the platform. "Pastor Jim," Tommy began, "there is someone here I'd like you to meet. Jack is a friend of ours from California. He is going to be staying with us in Carlisle for a week or so."

The pastor looked at Jack as if he recognized him. *Was that my imagination?* Jack wondered.

The preacher smiled at him. "Nice to meet you, Jack. Don't listen to any long stories Tommy has to say about me. He has a wild imagination." He chuckled. Sally laughed, with an *I told you* look.

"So I've heard," Jack replied. Tommy gave them the most innocent expression possible. Several people in the group smiled. "Jim has been our acting pastor the last half year while we search for someone to fill the spot permanently. Jack pastors a church in California," he added.

Jack's hope of remaining anonymous wasn't working out so well.

"Jack Hamilton of Living Valley Church!" Jim exclaimed triumphantly. "I thought you looked familiar! I recognize your voice now. What brings you to our corner of the world?"

Jack explained about the transmission problem with his vehicle. "I pulled into Tommy's Texaco station, and the rest is history."

"I know it may be a little inconvenient for you, Pastor Jack, but we are delighted to have you here with us. We sell a couple of your books in our bookstore. I listen to your radio broadcast all the time."

I guess there's nowhere I can hide, Jack thought. "Please, call me Jack," he said.

"Jack, we want to take you out for a Texas-size steak lunch. We're going to show you some *real* Southern hospitality. Tommy hasn't been starving you at his place, has he?" he asked sarcastically. Sally smiled.

"He has a hollow leg just like me, Jim. The boy is amazing." Jim introduced his wife, Penny, and their three children, Tina, Angie, and Blake. He also met Andrew and

Debra Johnson. Andy was an accountant and church elder. Jim motioned to a lady in the group.

"There is one more person on our staff I would like you to meet, Jack. This is Cynthia. She's our church secretary."

"Nice to meet you, Pastor Jack," she said with an exquisite, melodic voice. As Jack took her hand, he couldn't help staring at the beautiful young woman before him. She wore a long blue silk dress, dangling black earrings, and elegant black leather shoes to match. She had creamy white skin with a soft smattering of freckles that added another layer of beauty. Her warm blue eyes were accentuated by her light brown hair with natural gold streaks. Jack noticed small black specks in her eyes, and then quickly looked away.

A man could drown in those blue eyes, he thought.

"Nice to meet you, Cynthia," Jack replied politely. A young boy stood next to her. "This is my son, Timothy," she said, smiling with maternal pride. The boy beamed as Jack shook his hand as well. Cynthia slipped her arm around Timothy and gave him a hug. It was time enough for Jack to notice the conspicuous absence of a wedding band.

Elder Tommy redirected the conversation. "Now that all the introductions have been made, how about we go get a bite to eat? This hollow leg of mine is empty."

* * * * * * *

Jim wouldn't let Jack order anything smaller than a sixteen-ounce rib-eye for lunch. He didn't have room for dessert after steak, a loaded baked potato, and vegetables. The fellowship was wonderful. Over lunch Jack learned about events at the church. Things were in a state of transition. Jim Blevins had been the associate pastor for the last twelve years, since the church was founded in fact. He assumed the position of interim senior pastor after Dwight Atkins, Cynthia's husband, died unexpectedly from a heart attack eight months ago. Jack looked over at Cynthia and Timothy sympathetically. He now knew the whole story.

Jim agreed to stay on as interim senior pastor until a replacement could be found. His own father's health back in Mississippi was failing, however. Jim, Penny, and the children were planning on moving back to Jacksonville as soon as a new senior pastor could be found. A large number of candidates had already been interviewed, and several prospective ministers had preached on Sunday mornings for them. However, it had been the consensus of the board that they had not yet seen the right person, and they needed to find that person soon. Jim's family could not afford to be delayed much longer given his father's failing health.

"That's where you come in, Jack," Jim smiled.

Jack almost spilled the ice water he was drinking. "Me? What do you mean, *that's where I come in?*"

The adults looked at him with knowing smiles, as if he was the only one clueless about what was happening. They had that *you are the answer to prayer* look about them.

"Jack, we want you to be our interim senior pastor for the next three months, starting with Sunday service next weekend. My father has just been released from ICU, and I have to get back to Jacksonville and help care for him for a while." They all looked at him in agreement.

This can't be really happening, he thought to himself.

"That's it?" Jack said incredulously. "I drive into town one day and you want to make me your interim pastor the next?" He detected the upward curl of a playful smile growing on Tommy Smith's face. He knew he was about to say something.

"Yeah. That's about right, Pastor Jack. We all know who you are. You are more qualified than anyone we have interviewed for the job. Heck, you can probably run our church with one hand tied behind your back *and* blind-folded coming from that big church of yours in California."

Jack didn't like where this discussion was going. He felt ambushed and cornered. Then a thought came to him.

"That's just it. I can't stay. I have to get back to that church in California," he said with less conviction than he intended. Somehow, he knew God was in on this siege. If that were the case, he knew there would be no way out. He thought he could sense the Lord laughing at his predicament. Tommy confirmed his suspicions.

"Last I heard, you took a three-month leave of absence from Living Valley Church and canceled all your speaking engagements for a month. What do you say, Pastor Jack?" They all looked at him expectantly.

Jack, like the prophet Jonah, knew resistance to the will of God was futile, and risky. He had to ask one thing before pulling out the white flag. "How about my speaking engagements?"

"Not a problem as long as you're back for Sunday service," Jim replied with a smile. "Cynthia will take all calls and run the office while you're gone."

Jack scanned the faces of everyone at the table. He saw hope and expectation on their faces. He certainly wasn't expecting this when he pulled into Carlisle, Texas. Only God could have conjured up such an outrageous scenario. He took a deep breath.

"Very well," he said. "I agree to be your pastor during my leave of absence from Living Valley," he said with resignation. They all applauded and cheered. Jack Hamilton, city slicker from Los Angeles, could hardly believe the words that just came out of his mouth. He was going to be the pastor of a cowboy church for the next quarter year. He just had to know one last thing. "Do I have to wear cowboy boots?"

* * * * * * *

Word spread like wildfire. Jack Hamilton was pastoring the Cowboy Church in Carlisle, Texas. People from the surrounding area came to hear him speak. People who knew Jack drove two hours from Texas and Arkansas to hear him. Jack thought his sister Dorothy in Tennessee might be upset at him for committing to stay in Texas. She laughed when he told her about his predicament. She had to fly down from Nashville to visit him and see things for herself.

Meanwhile, church attendance was skyrocketing. A second Sunday morning service had to be added to accommodate the crowds. It was somewhat comical to see Jack pull into the senior pastor parking space of the Cowboy Church in his blue mica Lexus ISF.

Jack was still preaching in his slacks and Italian leather shoes. He was reluctant to buy cowboy boots. Doing so, he reasoned, might make everyone think he was planning on staying permanently, and that was something he just wasn't able to wrap his head around.

* * * * * * *

"Those are beautiful horses," Jack said, looking out the kitchen window of the Smiths sprawling ranch home.

Tommy eyed his animals affectionately, sipping a tall glass of lemonade during the church cook-out in Jack's honor a month after his arrival. "Yes they are," he agreed.

"I have every kind of animal you can think of on my ranch. Cows, chickens, pigs, and dogs. You name it. But the horses are my favorite," he said, pointing to several magnificent steeds close to the house. He pulled a bag of baby carrots from the refrigerator and gave it to Jack. "Here. Take this out to them. They're friendly. They'll come right up to the fence and eat out of your hand."

"Thanks, Tommy. I would enjoy that immensely," Jack said, as he stepped outside and headed toward the horses some forty yards away. A few horses lifted their heads and ambled over to the fence as he approached.

From the porch, Tommy watched with a smile. *The man deserves some peace after everything he's been through,* he thought. Jut then, he heard voices behind him and turned to see Sally and Cynthia walking toward him.

"There you are, girls. Cynthia, do me a favor." Tommy poured a tall glass of ice-cold lemonade from a pitcher and handed it to her." Jack is feeding the horses. Would you take this lemonade out there to him. I know he would appreciate it greatly."

Cynthia agreed without a second thought. She set out in Jack's direction with the lemonade wearing blue jeans, cowgirl boots, and a soft yellow blouse. Tommy and Sally watched her approach Jack and the horses through their large kitchen window.

"They make a really nice couple, don't you think?" Tommy asked Sally.

She raised a brow and eyed him suspiciously. "Tommy Smith, what are you up to?" she said warily.

Her suspicions grew along with the mischievous smile on his face. "Why, nothing, dear. I just thought Jack was getting thirsty and needed something to drink, that's all."

Sally huffed. She had known Tommy Smith since she was eight years old. There was more going on in that head. He'd let her in on his little agendas sooner or later. It didn't take long.

"Do you remember the first time I asked you out on a date?" he said, knowing full well she did. He continued before she could reply. "I was having dinner at Joe's Steakhouse, and you were my waitress. You brought me a tall glass of lemonade and I was hooked from that moment on. There's just something about a pretty girl with a tall glass of lemonade," he said, as he put an arm around his wife. Sally sank into her husband's warm embrace with a smile of surrender as she had done so many times over the years. She watched Cynthia hand Jack the tall glass of lemonade, bringing back a flood of memories. *Jack doesn't have a chance,* she thought to herself.

****

Tommy was right. These horses are friendly, Jack thought as he fed them their customary snack. Just then, the horses, movements told him that someone was approaching. He turned and saw Cynthia walking toward him with a tall beverage. She smiled and greeted him as she approached. "Hi, Pastor Jack. Tommy asked me to bring this to you. He thought you might be thirsty. It's hard work feeding horses carrots, you know," she said sarcastically.

He laughed, welcoming the company. "It is," he said, playing along. "I don't know how Tommy manages." He gratefully accepted the lemonade and took three large gulps. "I could get used to this," he said, smiling, holding up the tall glass.

"I know what you mean. Country life is all I have ever known," she said in her beautiful Southern twang. "I used to barrel race before Timothy was born. I was pretty good at it too."

Jack looked at Cynthia with admiration. "That's remarkable. How long have you lived here in Carlisle?"

Cynthia grabbed some carrots from his bag and started feeding a brown mare. "Dwight and I moved here twelve years ago from Amarillo to start this church. We've been here ever since. He always wanted to be a pastor, and I always wanted to be a pastor's wife."

Jack shook his head slightly and looked down to the ground. "You lost your husband and you *always* wanted to be a pastor's wife. I lost my wife and she *never* wanted to be a pastor's wife. Pretty ironic, wouldn't you say?"

"I loved Dwight. I never expected him to die so young. I'm sure your situation came as a big surprise as well," she said, staring into the distance.

"It was a very painful surprise. After my wife left, I received dozens of marriage proposals. Some from women in my congregation and some by letter from women I had never even met. I guess that's what happens when your personal life is headline news. There's not much I can do about it," he said. There was a brief silence. Jack picked up the conversation again. "So what are your plans?"

"I'm not sure yet. Dwight's parents live in Carlisle, but my family is back in Amarillo. I would like to be closer to them, and I know Tim would like that too. He's home schooled, so nothing is really keeping us here. Of course, I'll stay until a new senior pastor is settled in. Now that Jim and his family are moving back to Mississippi in a couple of months, we will have to have someone in place soon."

"Staying here is out of the question, I suppose?" Jack asked.

"It would be awkward for me as the former pastor's wife to remain at the church. And frankly, I don't have any other good reason to stay.

Jack looked into Cynthia's sad blue eyes. "No admirer keeping you here either?" he ventured. "Surely you must have some of those."

"There were some at first, but I ran them off. It was too soon.

I wasn't ready. No one has expressed any interest lately," she confided, her hands resting on the wooden fence.

"Maybe you would allow me to be the first?" Jack asked, placing a hand over hers. She did not draw away. A faint smile appeared on her face.

"I would like that," she replied softly. Jack squeezed her hand, holding the tall glass of lemonade in the other. His beverage may have been cold, but he radiated warmth from head to toe.

Tragedy had somehow brought them both to this point. He had no idea where God would lead them from here, but that didn't seem to be an issue. He was holding the hand of a beautiful young woman and in this magical moment nothing else really mattered. *Lord, help me,* he prayed silently.

* * * * * * * *

The next three months went by quickly. Jack fulfilled his commitment and his time in Carlisle, Texas, had come to a close. He was expected back in Los Angeles by the end of the week. He had told the staff at the Cowboy Church as much. The church board invited Jack to a meeting in the main sanctuary. Pastor Jim and Penny were there, as well as Andrew and Debra Johnson, Tommy and Sally Smith. Another couple Jack had met, David and Nicole Ingram, were also present. Cynthia was there as well, a little uncertain and nervous perhaps. They all sat around in a large circle. There was an empty seat reserved for him. *Perhaps they want my input on their selection of a candidate for senior pastor,* he thought to himself.

Pastor Jim began the meeting. "Jack, we thank God for sending you here during our transition period. We also thank you for your willingness to serve here for the last three months. You have touched and blessed many lives during your stay."

Jack was moved by their sincerity. He had grown very fond of the people in the church as well as in the community. "Thank you for making me feel so welcome. I have enjoyed my stay immensely. It will stay with me the rest of my life."

Tommy Smith cleared his throat, which meant he was about to speak.

"You know, Jack, I was praying for our new senior pastor when you pulled up to my gas station in your Lexus. I never thought I would get Jack Hamilton as an answer to prayer."

"Neither did I," replied Jack, laughing. Everyone else did the same. Tommy continued after the mirth subsided.

"We know you are supposed to go back to California, but we would be remiss if we failed to ask. *You* are the board's unanimous choice for senior pastor. We would like to offer you the position."

There was a moment of total silence. Jack didn't know what to expect at this meeting. He was used to that by now, though. Where God was concerned, Jack had learned to expect the unexpected. Everyone in the circle looked at Jack, waiting for his reply, knowing it would take a miracle for him to stay.

"I'll stay on one condition," he replied solemnly. Everyone looked at him quizzically. What could that be? Was it money? They could only pay him so much.

Tommy, with his deep Southern voice and perfect timing interjected, "Speak up, man! What is it?" All eyes were glued on Jack.

Jack sat in his chair, hands on his thighs, chuckling at Tommy's flair for the dramatic. "Very well," he said, standing up. He walked across to the opposite end of the circle and stood in front of Cynthia. She was a bit surprised when he gazed down at her with such obvious affection. Jack never took his eyes off her as he addressed the group. "I'll take the job as long as the girl comes with it." All eyes shifted from Jack to Cynthia. He knelt down before her and pulled out a small box and opened it, revealing an exquisite diamond engagement ring. He took the ring out of the box and offered it to her, saying, "Cynthia, will you marry me?"

Cynthia put a hand over her lips, tears streaming down her face. She nodded and stretched out a nervous, trembling hand to his. Jack held her soft, warm hand and delicately slipped the jewel band on her ring finger. He then took her in his arms and embraced her lovingly.

****

The double cabin pick-up cruised down the two-lane highway on a moonlit Texas night. Jack drove with his left hand on the steering wheel and his right arm around the shoulders of the cowgirl by his side. He was feeling more like a Texan every day. He stepped on the gas in his ostrich-skin boots, wearing Levi jeans, a long-sleeve shirt, and a wide belt with the name Jack across the back. They were on their way to dinner and the rodeo, while Timothy spent the night with his grandparents.

Four months had passed since Jack decided to stay in Carlisle. He still had ties in Los Angeles, but this was home now. As they passed the church, a beacon of light shone down over the statue of the cowboy kneeling before a cross with a horse by his side. Cynthia snuggled beside Jack, eyes closed, smiling. He gave her a gentle squeeze. He looked at the statue with amazement. "You just never know what will happen when you walk into a cowboy church," he said with a smile.

The Damsel in Distress

It was another busy day in the office of this OB/GYN physician. OB/GYN stands for Obstetrician-Gynecologist. Allow me to explain to you what that *really* means. You see, an OB/GYN is the most poorly understood individual in the medical field. In order to prove this to you, I must clarify some misconceptions about my specialty.

Misconception #1: An OB/GYN has a regular day job and only sees patients in the clinic. Ha! Some people think an OB/GYN only sees pregnant women in the office and that's all we do. No big deal. There's a little more to it than that. We are also responsible for *catching the baby*. Hence, we are up at all hours because women's uteruses contract the most in the middle of the night. Don't ask me why this is the case. I can't wait to get to heaven and ask. Regardless, I spend long hours away from home and family waiting to catch the baby.

Misconception #2: An OB/GYN just shows up at the last minute to catch the baby. I wish it were that simple. One OB/GYN supervises Labor and Delivery and Antepartum/Postpartum Ward similar to a medicine doctor who runs an ICU or a trauma doctor who work in the ER. Sometimes there are multiple women in labor at the same time, some screaming at the top of their lungs until their little one is born. Then the babies take over the screaming duties. The next day we must see all the new moms on our rounds. At our hospital the OB/GYN also takes care of the circumcision on the newborn males.

L&D is an interesting place, to be sure. I have delivered as many as eight babies in one evening during my practice. Sometimes that translates into little to no sleep. Furthermore, catching the baby is not always that simple. Occasionally we have to use forceps or a vacuum extractor to get the baby out. Yes, it really is called a *vacuum extractor*. Sometimes a woman will labor all night and then have to undergo a cesarean section (C-section). This leads me to misconception number three.

Misconception #3: An OB/GYN is not a surgeon. Try telling a woman who has ever had a C-section she didn't really have surgery and see what she says. Yes, OB/GYNs are surgeons, even though people don't always think of us as such. In addition to performing C-sections (the most common surgery in the country), we also repair lacerations and episiotomies after a natural birth. We also perform other common operations such as hysterectomies, tubal ligations, and D&C (dilation and curettage). So, besides seeing patients in Clinic, ER, ICU, Med-Surg, L&D, Antepartum/Postpartum, and the Nursery, our tour of the hospital would not be complete without time in the OR.

In summary, an OB/GYN is kind of a jack-of-all-trades in the medical field. We do a little bit of everything at all hours. We see patients in the office, deliver babies, and perform surgeries. Most OB/GYNs are very busy people. I share all that to say this: it was just another *busy* day in the office of this OB/GYN when patient DD (Damsel in Distress) walked in for her appointment.

She was a very pleasant lady in her late thirties. She had driven two hours for this consultation visit. I began taking a medical history and learned that she had been dealing with irregular bleeding and pain for years. Multiple medical therapies had been tried by primary doctors without success.

She and her husband were at their wit's end. While her husband sat in the waiting room, the lady continued her story. She had already had her tubes tied and was no longer interested in fertility. After nineteen years in practice, I already knew what to say next.

"Well, ma'am," I started, "I believe you would benefit from a hysterectomy."

"Oh, thank you!" she gasped. "I have been trying to get one for several years. When can we do the surgery? The sooner the better!"

We reached a point in the doctor's visit I don't always look forward to: scheduling. This is the part where I have to break the news to the patient about my sometimes long waiting list. "Well...," I began cautiously, "I'm a busy surgeon, and this is one of the busiest times of the year for me. The earliest I could possibly do your surgery would be in three to four months." My words came out as hollow as bamboo. I waited to see what her response would be. Some people don't mind the wait for elective surgery, while others don't take the news so well. This patient exploded into uncontrollable sobbing.

"You mean I have to live with this for *three to four more months?*" she asked, tears streaming down her face. I handed her a Kleenex. If there is one thing most men can't stand, it's to see a woman cry. Worse than that, to see a woman cry because of something *you said.* All I needed now was for her mascara to start running for me to feel lower than an alligator. She'd been dealing with this problem for years, driven all that distance in search of help, and now I'd dashed her hopes and made her cry. I sat there in my office frustrated and helpless.

Surely there is something you can do, I thought to myself. *There's always something you can do!* It would require making my busy OR schedule even busier, but the honorable, noble, gallant, and all-around nice guy doctor in me had to at least go through my OR schedule calendar to see if there was anywhere I could add her hysterectomy, a major case. As I suspected, my calendar was booked for the next three to four months. Her tears continued. I put my left hand to my forehead with aggravation as I continued searching my schedule for a solution.

I looked at my log more closely and came up with an idea. "I'll tell you what I can do," I said. "I have an OR day next month with all minor surgeries. I will move a minor surgery to another day, and we can put your hysterectomy on the schedule for that day." This would take some coordination and make that OR day even busier, but what else could I do? Chivalry demanded I do *something*.

"Oh thank you! You have no idea how much this means to me," she said, tears still running down her cheeks, this time with joy. She was obviously very grateful that I had made an extra effort to help with her problem. She continued to thank me profusely while I proceeded to add to an already full OR schedule with resignation. After two decades helping relieve patients' suffering, I was used to this sort of thing, even though it would cost me something in the process.

"You're welcome," I replied. "What can I say? I'm a sucker for a damsel in distress." Don't ask me why I made this admission after two decades of practice. I suppose succumbing to her passionate plea for help would not be complete without a confession on my part. She laughed amidst the watery eyes and smeared mascara. That smile on my patient's face made it all worthwhile.

That evening I shared the *damsel in distress* story with my wife over dinner. "You did the right thing, honey," she said. I agreed.

I like to think I did my part to ensure chivalry lives on. I suppose, therefore, I will always be a sucker for the damsel in distress.

The Double X Factor

Mankind's greatest unsolved mystery does not even have a name or definition. And yet, it has eluded man's greatest efforts to understand and explain it. It has been a source of great confusion, perplexity, and frustration over the centuries for people from every civilization and continent on the face of the earth. In exasperation, men who have not been able to figure it out have proclaimed, "Women! You can't live with them, and you can't live without them!" Those *unique qualities* that men don't understand and can sometimes drive them wild can't be defined so I am proposing a new term for this unsolved mystery. I call it the Double X Factor.

Now don't confuse the Double X Factor with the more commonly known X Factor. Dictionary.com defines the noun X Factor as follows: *a hard to describe influence or quality; an important element with unknown consequences; also written X-Factor.* **Example.** *The new center on the basketball team is the X Factor.*

I define the Double X Factor as follows: *an impossible to describe influence or quality in women; a unique element with mysterious, unknown, and powerful consequences brought about by the female gender; also written Double X Factor. Example. Helen was the Double X Factor responsible for the Trojan War.*

There are several theories about contributing factors responsible for the Double X Factor phenomenon. Some say it's *hormonal* in nature. While it is true that women with functional ovaries produce large amounts of hormones, particularly estrogen, there is more to it than that. Puberty, ovulation, pregnancy, postpartum, PCOS, PMS, peri-menopause, and menopause are all terms you are familiar with. Some or all of these conditions are experienced by women during the course of their hormonal life. As an OB/GYN physician, I help care for women during these different seasons. Estrogens may be some of the most powerful molecules on earth, but they are *not* the primary cause of the Double X Factor.

Then there are those who say the Double X Factor is primarily *environmental*. This theory simply states that your surroundings and upbringing help shape ideas and behaviors; for example, the type of family, educational, and cultural experiences you grew up with.

There is one more theory out there that must be mentioned in order to make this brief discussion on causes of the Double X Factor complete. Some theorize that the Double X Factor is primarily due to *psychosocial* factors. As you have probably surmised, this deals with a combination of psychological and social factors in varying degrees, hence the term *psychosocial*. It's a popular and catchy phrase we use in the medical literature to help describe multi-factorial things we really don't have a good handle on. You will probably never see this phrase again outside of a medical journal or the final question on an episode of the television game show *Jeopardy*. I am mentioning this in case you make it as a finalist on the latter. You can thank me later.

While hormonal, environmental, and psychosocial factors no doubt play a part in shaping female attributes, we have to dig a little deeper to get to the root of the issue. As such, you have to know some basic genetics in order to understand how the phrase Double X Factor came about. In simple terms, all cells in the human body (except sperm and eggs) contain twenty-three pairs for a total of forty-six chromosomes. Women have 46 XX and men have 46 XY number of chromosomes.

Woman, like man, was created in the image of God in the beginning.[1] They are a three-part being, possessing a spirit, soul, and body. There is no difference between men and women in the spirit, as far as God is concerned.[2] The only difference between males and females exists at the molecular level. Hence, the Double X Factor manifests itself in the body and soul of a female. The soul refers to the mind, will, and emotions. The minute distinction is the fact that females have one more tiny X chromosome instead of the Y chromosome in males. That little, itsy-bitsy extra X chromosome God gave Eve in the Garden of Eden in His infinite wisdom is responsible for the phenomenon that makes "women" women. Hence the Double X Factor.

The Double X Factor has shaped the course of history more than any other single entity in the world. More than natural disasters, science, music, art, psychology, and philosophy combined. The Double X Factor can be summed up in one word: *power*. Undeniable, irresistible, and unstoppable power. It is more powerful than the atomic bomb. It is more powerful than a locomotive, speeding bullet, and Superman himself. All Lois Lane has to do is cry for help once or flutter those long, pretty eyelashes to bring the man of steel flying in at supersonic speed. How is this possible, you ask? Remember, it is the neck that turns the head. The Double X Factor has shaped the course of history.

Consider how Eve in the Garden of Eden was deceived by the serpent. He talked her into eating from the tree of the

Knowledge of Good and Evil.[3] *She also gave to her husband with her, and he ate.* This one decision by Eve—the original Double X woman—led to the fall of mankind. Don't get me wrong, ladies. I am not picking on Eve. In her defense, Satan took advantage of that part of her beautiful, merciful, delicate, and innocent naiveté that gives others the benefit of the doubt more than men. He took advantage of her Double X Factor.

How about Sarai (who later became Sarah) persuading Abram (who later became Abraham) to have a child by her Egyptian maid Hagar instead of trusting God to keep His promise? In a moment of wavering faith, Sarai unduly influenced her husband. Abram *heeded the voice of Sarai.* He went in to Hagar, and she conceived and bore a son named Ishmael. This was the start of a large family feud that continues to this day.[4] Abram, the father of our faith, was influenced by the Double X-Factor.[5]

How about Esther, who persuaded King Ahasuerus to deliver her people, the Jews, from total annihilation when all hope seemed lost? An irreversible decree in the laws of the Persians and Medes had gone out that all the Jews in the empire should be destroyed on the thirteenth day of the twelfth month, which is the month of Adar. Esther was able to rescue her people from destruction. How did she accomplish this? With a few well-timed feasts for the king, exposing wicked Haman's plot that got him hanged, a few decrees allowing the Jews to defend themselves, and declaring Purim a national holiday still celebrated today.[6] Piece of cake. No big deal for a woman who possesses the Double X Factor.

Hopefully, you are starting to understand the magnitude of power wielded by those who possess the Double X. You may not think of women as *the weaker sex* anymore. If you are still a little skeptical, just ask Samson.[7] Delilah defeated him with ease where a thousand Philistine warriors failed miserably. The name Delilah still echoes through the hallways of history and has anchored itself in the subconscious of males over the centuries with weary respect. How many men do you know who have named *their* daughters Delilah? Ask any man who has ever watched the movie *Fatal Attraction*. Ask any male black widow spider who has survived his honeymoon. What is the take-home message here, guys? Don't mess with the Double X!

Please do not misunderstand me. I am not saying the Double X Factor is a *bad* thing. On the contrary. I am of the opinion that the Double X Factor is a *good* thing when in the right hands and used with good intentions. In fact, when He created mankind, God intended for the Double X-Factor to be a good thing. When God saw everything that He had made, indeed it was *very good*.[8] Let me give you several reasons why the Double X Factor is very good. Let's go back to where it all began, in the Garden of Eden.

Reason #1: You wouldn't be here if not for the Double X Factor. After the Lord made Adam and Eve, He said to them, "Be fruitful and multiply."[9] Without the Double X Factor, there would be no multiplication, or reproduction. None of us would be here. It takes someone with two X chromosomes to conceive and give birth to a human being. Have you hugged your Double X mom lately?

Reason #2: There would be no marital sex without the Double X. Sex is not a dirty word, not even close. Instead it was a stroke of genius by our Creator. It was God's idea for a husband and wife to be part of the marriage relationship. Remember "be fruitful and multiply." Sex was not only God's *idea* for a healthy marriage; it was a *command* for a healthy marriage. I am convinced there would be more harmony in the home if husbands would just have more sex with their Double X.

Reason #3: The Double X Factor is there to compliment her husband. *The LORD God said, "It is not good that man should be alone; I will make him a helper comparable to him."*[10]

One of the most intriguing things about the Double X Factor is that it has many subtle and unique qualities. How is it, for example, that a man can spend fifteen minutes (and he will) looking in the refrigerator for the mustard and not find it? His wife walks by, sticks her hand amidst the myriad of jugs, cartons, and bottles, and pulls out a yellow mustard container in no time. He looks at her incredulously and asks, "How did you do that!" A wife never answers that question. She just walks away with a knowing smile on her face. I know how the guy feels.

My wife, Libby, and I were going down the road in a car the other day. She was driving while I was in the passenger seat, digging through her purse for a pen to write something down. I jokingly call her purse *the black hole*, a place where things go in but never come out. I spent five minutes looking through the black hole for the pen my wife promised me was *in there somewhere*.

"I know it's there, honey," she said to me, keeping her eyes on the road. I stuck my hand in the black hole again and searched a couple more minutes, to no avail. Finally, I gave up in frustration.

"Let me try," she said to me while driving. Then she inserted her right hand blindly into her purse with her eyes fixed on the road.

"It's not in there. I have searched everywhere," I replied confidently. No way was there a pen in that purse! And yet… she fumbled around in her bag for less than five seconds and pulled out a pen!

I looked over at her, eyes and mouth agape with

amazement, wondering where she came by those amazing super powers. "How did you do that!" I exclaimed, but she didn't answer, just kept driving with that knowing smile on her face.

I'm convinced that incidents like these have been played out repeatedly in households around the world throughout history. These abilities are a well-kept secret among women. They only talk about them when men are not around. However, they do teach them to their daughters at an early age. I have three daughters. I have lived this. I know what I'm talking about.

All they have to do is walk into the room, fidgeting with their hands, batting their eyelashes, and saying *Daddy*. No man alive is immune to this stealthy approach. We know it's coming and we steel ourselves against the overpowering urge to cave in—but the reality is that we are helpless to do anything but concede. They look up to us with those beautiful, pleading, sometimes watery eyes and we know we don't have a chance. Then their lips quiver ever so slightly, and we raise the white flag of surrender! Yes, fathers know the power of the Double X Factor all too well.

Perhaps we men should take a moment to consider the possibility that God is trying to teach us something. These are my thoughts on the subject.

The Double X Factor God has placed in every woman is beautiful. It is the Double X Factor that gives women their unsurpassed mystery, fascination, and charm. It is a fragrance gifted to them by a loving and masterful Creator. When tenderly fertilized, watered, and nurtured, the Double X Factor blooms into a flower of unsurpassed grace, eloquence, and beauty. Men often go to museums in search of beauty, while missing the beauty right beside them. Husbands, take a look at your wives. Fathers, take a look at your daughters. Ladies, take a look at yourselves in the mirror. What do you see? The Double X Factor is in there and it is one of God's greatest gifts to mankind. Thank you, Lord, for the Double X Factor. Where would we be without it?

[1]Genesis 1:1, 27
[2]Galatians 3:28
[3]Genesis 3:1–6
[4]Genesis 16:1; 21:1–21
[5]Romans 4:9–18
[6]Esther 1–9
[7]Judges 13–16
[8]Genesis 1:31
[9]Genesis 1:28
[10]Genesis 2:18

The Drama Queen

Nikolas Adrinov walked into the fine jewelry store that evening on a mission of closure. He was greeted by the familiar faces of the store manager, Ms. Walker, and her assistant, Tiffany. There were other customers in the store, but the young entrepreneur was by far their best.

Nikolas had frequented the Gem River on a regular basis over the years, paying cash for the many purchases he made for the ladies in his life. He was a generous man who relished giving women gifts of jewelry as much as they relished receiving them. Through the years, he had purchased every kind of jewel and precious stone. These ranged from citrine, garnet, rubellite, chalcedony, and peridot, to opal, tourmaline, pearls, sapphires, and diamonds. This was the first time he had returned a purchase.

Nikolas walked into the store and looked around for Angela, the pleasant but simple young lady who had assisted him with his purchases for the past few years. She was very knowledgeable about gems and had exquisite taste. All his lady friends loved her selections. Nikolas trusted her implicitly. Spotting her in the back of the store, he made a straight line for her. Looking up from the glass pane and seeing him coming, she greeted Nikolas with her best smile. "Hello, Mr. Adrinov," she said respectfully.

"Good evening, Angela. You are very kind, but please call

me Nikolas," he insisted. Being called *Mr. Adrinov* by Angela always made him feel old when in fact he was only several years her senior.

"Very well—Nikolas. What can we do for you this evening?" she asked politely.

Nikolas pulled out a small black box and set it on the counter. He opened the box to reveal a brilliant five-carat engagement ring. "I am here to return this," he replied.

Angela looked at the beautiful ring with surprise. "Oh Mr. Nikolas! I am so sorry. Didn't she like the ring I chose for her?"

Nikolas grimaced at that.

"No, Angela. I wish it were that simple. The ring is wonderful. It's *me* she turned down. Two days ago for the man I thought was my best friend. You know, I thought she was the one I would spend the rest of my life with," he confided. Angela was touched by the pang of sadness in his voice.

Nikolas had shown Angela a picture of the woman for whom the ring was intended when he made the purchase. She was a stunning, tall, sophisticated-looking blond woman. She and Nikolas seemed to make a perfect match, but now it seemed the young beauty had other plans.

"We will certainly take the ring back and refund your money, Mr. Nikolas," she assured him. There was a brief silence. "I'm sure you will find the perfect person to settle down with one day," she said, trying to comfort the sad millionaire. She was genuinely concerned for him. Nikolas looked into her light green eyes and smiled.

"You make an excellent jeweler *and* therapist," he replied jokingly. Angela blushed and laughed at that. It was a sweet, melodious sound that permeated the air. For the first time in all the years she had been serving him, he saw her differently, realizing that she was no "plain Jane." There was more substance and intrigue to the woman standing before him than he had ever paused to consider. "Tell me, Angela," he said playfully. What wedding ring would you chose if *you* were married and money was no object?"

Angela was surprised by the question. Was he teasing her? Nikolas had asked her before which piece of jewelry *she* would choose when helping him decide, but today's circumstances were different. *Perhaps he is just trying to make small talk,* she reasoned. She gave him a smile and then began pondering his question, picturing all the exquisite rings in the store. Nikolas eyed her curiously, thinking she would select the most beautiful and expensive diamond ring in the shop. Cost was not an issue, after all.

After some fifteen seconds, Angela came to a decision. She looked up at Nikolas and smiled. "Follow me," she said playfully. Nikolas did so, a grin on his face. He was certain she would choose a ring even bigger and more costly than the one he returned—but he was wrong. Instead, Angela retrieved a plain, one-carat diamond, platinum arch ring with several small precious gems. It was worth a tenth of the value of the ring he was returning.

Nikolas was startled by her modest choice. He noticed a silver Ankh pendant hanging from her delicate neckline. Angela looked at the ring with a great deal of satisfaction.

"I like this one," she said with pleasure. "It is simple and elegant." Nikolas pondered her words in his mind. *Simple and elegant.*

* * * * * * *

Young Nikolas sat on the small sofa while his grandmother sat across him in her rocking chair, reading aloud from her

Bible. The warm summer sunlight shone through her modest apartment in Moscow. His parents had been killed in a terrible car accident six years earlier. Grandmother Sofiya had taken care of him since he was four years old. She read the Scriptures to him every day for an hour when he got home from school before he did his homework.

Little Nikolas never tired of hearing his grandmother read the Bible stories. Each time she taught him some new and exciting insight. She was old, wise, and very loving. He loved her dearly as well. Sofiya also taught him about life. Her words echoed in his mind at that moment.

"You must always be a gentleman, my dear boy. One day you will marry, Nikolas, and you must choose *very* carefully. It is one of the most important decisions you will ever make," she would say, putting a wrinkled hand on his knee. "Charm is deceitful and beauty is passing, my dear Nikolas.[1] True beauty comes from within. You want to marry a girl who is *simple and elegant.*"

* * * * * * *

Simple and elegant. Nikolas repeated the words to himself, as he looked into Angela's light green eyes, and then at the ring she had playfully slipped on her delicate finger. He looked at her with moist eyes and smiled, recalling Grandmother Sofiya's words from the past. "Simple and elegant," he said softly, repeating the words one last time. "I like that," he said, as Angela put the wedding ring away.

"Angela, it may seem awkward for me to ask you at this moment, but I must. Do you ever date a customer?" he inquired, almost pleading. Nikolas' question surprised her. His next question shocked her, momentarily leaving her at a loss for words. She had spent the last two years helping him choose jewelry for the many ladies he had dated, even proposed to. Now that Nikolas had recently been rejected, he was asking her to go out on a date with him.

Angela knew he was a gentleman. That was not the issue. But she couldn't help wondering if Nikolas was on the rebound and not genuinely interested in her. She couldn't tell for certain. So she looked into those handsome pleading gray eyes once more and realized she must know. "Maybe," she replied with a slight smile.

"Maybe?" he said.

"Maybe I would date a customer, if he were to come to one of my plays. I am finishing my master's degree in theatre, and I am currently directing my last play before I graduate, if you would be interested."

Nikolas chuckled. "I see. It seems I have no choice in the matter," he said with comical resignation. "Let the show begin," he said, smiling, and waving a hand in the air.

Angela giggled.

* * * * * * *

There were few empty seats in the university's performing arts auditorium. Nikolas watched the drama unfold before his eyes, the lights turned down. Angela, *his* Angela from the jewelry store, not only directed the play, she had written the script for *The Journey Home*. It was a moving story about an orphan boy's lonely journey through life until a loving family adopted him and gave him a home. By the time the last curtain went down, there wasn't a dry eye in the audience. The cast, including the writer and director, received a standing ovation. Later, he learned that she was affectionately called *the Drama*

Queen by her students. What a great misnomer, Nikolas thought, as he watched the Hispanic beauty wave at the audience, acknowledging their applause.

She found him in the audience, smiled, and waved joyfully. He smiled and waved back.

"Nikolas, I think you are in love with a Drama Queen," he whispered to himself jokingly. *What if she doesn't agree to go out with me after all?* He dared not entertain the thought.

* * * * * * *

The lady stood against the railing of the cruise liner looking at the sunrise. The warmth of the sun's rays, the fresh air, and the Greek islands surrounded her. She closed her eyes, basking in the moment. A few gray hairs were noticeable in an otherwise magnificent cascade of black hair. A handsome man in his fifties walked up behind her. She could hear him coming and kept her eyes closed.

"Good morning," said the familiar voice. He stood behind her, wrapping his arms around her in a blanket of affection, permeating her soul. He placed his head on her left shoulder, his head next to hers. His masculine aftershave still ignited her senses after all these years. She raised her left hand, gently caressing his cheek. On her ring finger, she wore a platinum arch ring with several small diamonds. *Simple and elegant.*

[1] Proverbs 31:30

The Exchange

Augustus sat quietly in his dungeon cell, his hands shackled to a stone wall. His eyes were closed as he tried to forget the physical and verbal abuse from his captors over the last few days. His tormentors came when he least expected them, always smiling, clearly enjoying his suffering. He hoped he would never become like them—cruel and merciless.

He longed to be free. *Will anyone rescue me?* he wondered. *Does anyone care?* Everyone has a breaking point, and he was sure he was approaching his. Hope seemed like a thing of the past. *What I wouldn't give to be free*, he thought to himself. *I would do anything in exchange for my freedom!*

Just then, he noticed a commotion in the corridor near his cell door. Two familiar figures appeared. Augustus thought they were back to torture him again, but he was surprised to discover otherwise. They were in a hurry. "Come with us!" said one of his keepers, as he was loosed from his shackles.

"Where are you taking me?"

"You are to be released. The price has been paid for your freedom," his captor muttered.

How is this possible? Who would do such a thing? I am just a lowly soldier in the kingdom's army, Augustus thought to himself. But the men seemed to mean business. They escorted him out of the pit and up to the surface.

Outside, Augustus witnessed two armies facing each other.

He belonged to the freedom army led by the man simply known as the General, who had never been defeated. The evil army was led by their grand marshal, the Dragon.

The men brought him to the open field between the two opposing forces, where they paused long enough for both sides to see who the men were holding. Then, his captors took Augustus to the Dragon and threw him to the ground at his side. The sinister leader looked down at Augustus with contempt. Clearly his life meant nothing to the evil grand marshal.

As Augustus lay there on the ground, the General approached the Dragon, accompanied by two of his officers. Although he didn't understand what was going on, Augustus smiled at the sight of his commander. The General glanced down at him, acknowledging him. Then the General and the Dragon squared off, facing each other.

"You know the terms," began the Dragon.

"Yes, I do," replied the General, "and I agree to them." Augustus couldn't help but wonder what terms they were talking about. "I would like a word in private with my soldier first," the General said.

His adversary looked annoyed, but agreed. With that, the General took several steps forward. Augustus' tormentors released him, and he gladly approached his commander.

"Augustus, I do not have much time. You must always remember what I tell you. I want you to know that you are valuable. The things the enemy has said to you are lies. You are as significant to me as any soldier in my army. There is greatness inside of you. I believe in you."

Augustus's former tormentors grabbed the General by the arms, but He offered no resistance. the Dragon had a sinister smile on his face, and his minions laughed, as they punched the General repeatedly. When he collapsed to the ground in front of Augustus, the former captive's joy turned to terror. He finally realized that an exchange had been made—the General's life for his!

"General, you cannot do this! Please! I am not worthy!" Augustus shouted.

"You are worth it to me, Augustus," the General answered. "Now you understand the price of freedom." The two soldiers picked the General up and led him to the enemy camp, beating and whipping him along the way.[1] It was around the ninth hour and there was darkness over the land.[2]

Augustus remained there on his knees in great despair. He could see the Dragon's feet in front of him. He looked up at his cruel eyes. "What are you going to do with your pathetic life now?" he asked, as he turned and walked away.

Things were different now. His General's enemy had become his enemy. Augustus stood to his feet. "I am going to spend my life setting people free from your clutches, in the name of my Lord."[3] the Dragon stopped briefly. Augustus turned and walked back toward his fellow soldiers.

"You don't have the guts!" yelled the Dragon.

"Watch me," he replied, without looking back.

[1] Isaiah 53:7–8
[2] Matthew 27:45
[3] 1 John 3:8

The Faith that Sees

John Sampson looked from his bedroom balcony across his sprawling estate. The sunset view from the upstairs was spectacular. The beautiful lawns, gardens, fountains, vineyards, and ponds all spoke one word. Wealth. John had wealth, and lots of it. He had spent his entire life working to achieve this material success. He was now taking a moment to survey the fruits of his labors from his private chamber.

He sat on his leather sofa as he gazed at his multi-million-dollar estate. His glass was still full of wine from his private collection. But even his best wine could not satisfy him tonight. He felt empty, very empty. He lived in a luxurious mansion with servants to tend to his every need, and yet there was no one to share his life with. He had no siblings, and his parents had died when he was just a boy. His wife of eleven years had grown tired of his obsession with money and divorced him. *The squirrels, rabbits, fish, ducks, and birds are enjoying my property more than I am,* he thought.

John stood on the peak of material success, looking down at all he had and feeling miserable. *Is this how it's supposed to feel?* he wondered. *Shouldn't I feel exhilarated when I think of all my accomplishments? Instead, I feel like a failure.*

John put his wineglass down on the night table. Then he sat down, closed his eyes, and began to ponder where his life had gone wrong. It was then that he heard something he had not heard in a very long time—God's still, small voice saying, "Give Me another chance, John. I love you still, and I can help you get your life back on track. I can help you remember what is really important."

John had always known about Jesus, but he couldn't say he had a relationship with Him. He had pushed all that aside in order to pursue wealth and what he thought would be happiness. But now, tonight, he knew he'd made a mistake. All those things he had held onto so tightly were not making him happy. Instead they left him feeling lonely and sad.

"Where do I start, Lord?" he whispered as he turned off the light.

The next day was Sunday, and John thought it might help to go to church. This time he vowed to have an open heart. It wasn't long until he made the decision to surrender his life to God. Why not, he'd tried it his own way. "I'll do what You ask of me," he told the Lord. "Just give me the grace to obey."

Soon after, he went to missions school training, and two years later, he left his luxurious mansion for a remote portion of Eastern Europe. His job was to teach English and feed and clothe the poor. He also provided basic medical care when possible. Much to his surprise, he found these tasks enriching. They brought him an inner joy he had never known. The townspeople were skittish at first, but with time they began to see that he genuinely cared for them. As their trust grew, they asked John to lead the Sunday morning church service.

One Sunday morning John's sermon was interrupted by an angry mob yelling behind the building. The group of fifty worshippers was shocked when the town's mayor and ten other men stormed into the meeting. Two of the men grabbed John and dragged him outside, where they tied his hands across the trunk of a nearby tree and ripped off his shirt. The men beat

John across his upper back with a thick rope. The first blow knocked him to his knees and took his breath away. John did his best to endure the excruciating pain, while his congregation watched in horror. Clearly the mayor was determined to let everyone know that he was in charge.

After ten lashes, the beating ended. The men cut John loose. John remained on the ground for a few moments composing himself, before picking up the Bible that had fallen to the ground as the men tied him to the tree. He picked it up, and rose to his feet.

"If you teach from that book again," the mayor yelled at him, "it will be worse for you! Do you understand me?"

John began to walk, and he didn't look back. He could feel the Bible in his hand and the wounds on his back. He was sure this encounter was only the first of many.

By the next weekend, John's friends were pleading with him not to preach. "The mayor hates Christians," they told him. "The mayor isn't about to stop persecuting you. You're just going to get hurt again."

John understood their apprehension, but he also knew he couldn't give up. "I must do this," he told them. Finally, they could see his resolve and said only, "The will of the Lord be done."[1]

When Sunday arrived, John was standing in the warehouse as usual, preaching to a slightly larger group than he had the week before. Some had come out of respect and others out of curiosity.

John preached on the love of God that morning. He was almost finished with his sermon when the mayor and his cronies interrupted again. Once again, John was led outside, his hands tied behind his back. He offered no resistance. This time they passed the tree and took him instead to an open field. While a growing crowd watched from a distance, the mayor's men forced John to his knees behind a small boulder and pinned the side of his head to the rock. The mayor stood near a bonfire in the center of the field, holding John's Bible in his hand.

"I told you not to teach from this book!" he exclaimed. "I warned you, but you wouldn't listen." With that, the mayor threw the Bible into the fire. Everyone heard the crackling of the fire and saw the Bible burning. They also saw a single page separate itself from the flames and gently land at the mayor's feet.

The mayor, whose name was Yakin, looked down at the piece of paper, picked it up, and surveyed it curiously. The page was blackened except for a few words in red. Yakin read the words out loud. "'Why are you persecuting Me?'"[2] The crowd stood in complete silence as he read the words again and again.

With his head still pressed against the stone, John said, "Your word shall not return to you void."[3]

Yakin looked at the piece of paper and then at John. He crumpled the page and threw it into the fire, and then ordered his men to put a hot iron to John's eyes. He was to be made blind.

Winter, with its bitter cold, came and went that year. It had been six months since the man of God had left town, blinded and broken. With the dawning of spring, word came that another man of God was coming to preach one night. The people wondered if this preacher would stay. After all, things had changed. They had a new mayor.

On the night of the service, the auditorium was packed with thousands of people from the town and surrounding villages. They all came for one thing, the preaching and teaching of the gospel. No one knew who the speaker was, but it didn't matter. The expectation in the air was electrifying.

The service started with several praise and worship songs, and then the new mayor entered the auditorium with his young daughter and the much-anticipated preacher, who was wearing dark glasses. The little girl looked up at the preacher and smiled. Then she led him by his left hand to the pulpit. Holding his Bible in his hand like a sword, he began to preach.

"'The Spirit of the LORD is upon Me, because He has anointed Me to preach the gospel to the poor...'"[4] For one power-packed hour, he preached on the fall of man, the cross, and salvation through faith in Jesus Christ. At the end of the sermon, the preacher invited people to come to the altar for prayer. Hundreds stood and started walking to the front. It was just then that a man raced ahead of everyone and threw himself in front of the preacher. The audience gasped and then fell silent.

The man was none other than Yakin, the old mayor.

With tears streaming down his face, he asked, "Can you forgive me?"

John paused for only a moment before saying, "You are forgiven." He then did the unthinkable. He stepped down and lifted his former adversary to his feet. He then embraced him. A mighty roar of approval rose from the crowd, followed by many expressions of praise to God.

A few weeks later John was at Yakin's house for a celebration. God had worked a great transformation in the former mayor's life. His bitter and cruel heart had been replaced with a tender one. There were about sixty of Yakin's relatives present at the party, some of whom had become believers in Jesus before Yakin's conversion.

"I knew you would one day come to the Lord," John told Yakin.

"What made you think so?" Yakin asked.

John answered with a smile, "God never fails." He then said to Yakin, "There's something I would like you to do for me."

"What is it?" Yakin responded.

"I want you to translate for me while I teach your family from the Bible," John told him.

Tearful and emotional, Yakin did not know what to say. What a great honor this would be. He called his relatives into the living room, old and young alike. He asked them to get comfortable and listen carefully—a great preacher was about to teach them. Then he seated John in a chair and sat down on the floor next to him.

When everyone was ready, John, still wearing his dark glasses, opened his Braille Bible and turned the pages. He arrived at the familiar passage of scripture with his fingertips and smiled. He began teaching his new disciples with these words: "'In the beginning God created the heavens and the earth.'"[5]

[1] Acts 21:12–14
[2] Acts 9:3–4
[3] Isaiah 55:11
[4] Luke 4:18–19
[5] Genesis 1:1

The Good-Looking Samaritan

The little orange coupe was on the side of the road, going nowhere. Like an open-mouth patient at the dentist's office, its hood was popped up for an expert to diagnose the condition. The only problem was that the lady in blue jeans and a pink T-shirt was no car doctor. She looked at the dead, unresponsive engine in despair. Was her Mazda in a coma or gone for good? She couldn't tell. All she knew was she needed a mechanic.

"What do I do now, furry rocket?" she asked the vehicle, as if it could talk. The car, with its plush seat covers, made no reply.

She heard a vehicle on the road pass her by and come to a halt on the gravel up ahead. Looking up, she watched as a tall, lean, muscular man wearing shorts, a polo shirt, and sports cap emerged from a white minivan and walked toward her.

Although she was eager for help, Jane was a little nervous. *I hope he stopped to help and he's NOT an axe murderer!* she thought. He looked okay. His dark tan and friendly smile began to melt away at her suspicions like the early morning sun. She was going to have to imagine what his eyes looked like behind his heavy shades.

"Looks like you could use some help," he said. "What seems to be the problem?"

"I don't know. It has been making a funny noise the last couple of days. I was going to take it to the shop on Monday and have it checked out," Jane replied. "I guess I pushed my luck too far this time."

The man leaned over the engine, checking a few things. Jane couldn't help but notice his muscular arms. His aftershave was doing a number on her, too. Dare she look to see if he wore a wedding band? Her blue eyes drifted down to his hand. No ring.

Then she quickly caught herself. *What am I thinking! I'm stranded on the side of the road with a total stranger. I should be on my guard.* But she was finding it difficult. Everything about this man exuded calmness, strength, and trust.

After jiggling some wires and taking a close look in some specific areas, the man gave Jane the bad news. "I'm sorry. I wish I could do more, but this is going to take more skill than I have. You need a real mechanic here." After standing there for an awkward moment, the man added, "Look, most of the auto shops around here don't open this early, but my brother-in-law Jared is a great guy and a really good mechanic. I could give him a call. He should be able to fix your car and have you back on the road in no time."

"Well, thank you, Mr.—" Jane started, not knowing his name.

"Dustin. Dustin Greer. Nice to meet you," he replied with a smile. "I haven't seen you around here before. You must be new to Dwaynesville," he added.

"I am, as a matter of fact," she said.

"Well, ma'am, you have nothing to worry about. People are very friendly and helpful here. I'll give Jared a call and see if he can come out and tow your car to his shop. He will be here in a few minutes to haul your car to his shop." Dustin pulled out his cell phone and made the arrangements.

"I'd be glad to give you a lift back to your place," Dustin

said. He could sense her reluctance to get into a car with a stranger. Anyone would feel that way.

"I'd better stay here and wait for the tow truck," she answered.

"I can't wait," he said. "I've got my girls in the car. But you could leave your key under the driver's floor mat. Your car will he safe here."

Just then, Jane heard the windows go down and two red-haired heads pop out. "Come on, Daddy. We're going to be late for the game," they called.

"I don't blame you for being a little hesitant about me giving you a ride. How many bad guys do you know take their girls to city-league soccer at seven forty-five on a Saturday morning?" he said, smiling.

"Oh, okay," she said finally. "Thank you."

As Jane climbed into the front passenger seat, she smiled at the two red-headed girls, wearing green soccer jerseys and seated in the back. They stared back.

"Girls, we have a guest riding with us today," he said. "Her name is—"

"Jane. Jane Stanley. Nice to meet you two," she said cheerfully. "Could you tell me your names?"

Dustin grinned as he closed the driver door, started up the engine, and pulled onto the highway.

"My name is Cara," said one girl, pointing to herself. "And this is my sister, Dara," she added.

"We're twins," Dara chimed in, smiling.

"I see that." Jane laughed, her hands on her lap. She couldn't tell them apart. "Let me guess. Cara was born first, because Cara comes before Dara," she said playfully.

"That's right!" they both said in unison. "Cara was born seven minutes before me," said Dara. "Do you have a middle name, Ms. Jane?" she continued.

"I don't have a middle name," she explained. "I guess you can say I am just *Plain Jane*." The girls giggled, making Jane smile. Her eyes met Dustin's.

There is absolutely nothing plain about this beautiful lady, he thought to himself. She smiled at him and turned her attention back to the girls. He didn't know much about his lovely new passenger. But one thing was clear. She was great with kids.

"Let me guess," Jane said. "You girls look like you're in the fourth grade."

"That's right!" said Cara. Dara was smiling in agreement.

"Who is your teacher's name?" she asked.

"We don't know yet. Mrs. Pruett, the old fourth-grade teacher, retired, and we haven't been told who is taking her place," Dara informed her.

"Well then, allow me to properly introduce myself," Jane said, placing a hand on her chest and fluttering her eyelids in feigned pomp and ceremony. "*I* am your new fourth grade teacher."

The girls started shouting for joy and clapping their hands excitedly. Dustin looked back at them again in his rearview mirror, chuckling. *I'm really going to enjoy the next parent-teacher conference,* he thought. Now it was his turn to see if she had a wedding ring. There was none. A small wave of relief and, was it *hope?* came over him.

Dara looked at the time on her watch. "Hurry, Daddy! It's almost eight o'clock. We're going to be late," she exclaimed somewhat anxiously. Dustin tried to put her at ease.

"Girls, Ms. Jane needs a ride home. We're going to drop her off at her apartment on the way to the soccer fields. That means we're going to be a little late this time. The Hawks are going to have to start without us, but it will all work out."

Jane immediately spoke up. "Oh, please. I don't want you to be late to your game on my account. I would be glad to go to the soccer field with all of you, if you don't mind dropping me off afterward."

The girls were delighted with Jane's idea. "Are you sure?" Dustin asked.

"Absolutely! I'm new around here. This is a great opportunity to see what goes on around her on the weekends," Jane replied.

Cara and Dara couldn't be happier. "We are going to show you off to the other fourth graders," Cara boasted.

"You're going to like our team. We're undefeated this season. We have won eight games in a row. Dad is the assistant coach," Dara added smiling proudly.

Jane looked up at Dustin. "Oh he is, is he? I must confess I don't know much about soccer," she added.

"I'll be glad to tell you whatever you want to know," he said softly.

* * * * * * *

"I thought you were the assistant coach," Jane said playfully. "Isn't the assistant coach supposed to be out there coaching?"

"I didn't think it would be right to leave you alone, watching in the bleachers, after everything you have been through this morning and new in town. Besides, Doris, the head coach, can handle things just fine without me today." Doris, a police dispatcher, was cheering the girls on passionately. They laughed at her shouting and gesturing, arms flying in all directions.

"I see what you mean," Jane admitted, chuckling at the

theater that is little league soccer. Several other matches were going on in adjacent fields.

There was a brief silence between them as they watched the twins, both forwards, trying to score a goal for their team. Then Jane asked what had happened to the girls, mother.

"Marsha died of leukemia a couple of years ago," he said softly. "The girls and I all miss her, but we choose to remember the good times we shared together."

"She must have been a special lady. You have two beautiful children and a wonderful family. I'm sure you will find someone else one day," Jane said, as someone who had known heartache and disappointment herself.

Her words hovered over Dustin like a cool, refreshing mist. *Someone…one day.* Was Jane that *someone?* Was today that *one day?*

Dustin and Jane carried on a lively conversation throughout the match. Cara and Dara waved at them at half-time. During the second half, Jane learned all about Franklin Elementary and Dwaynesville. Dustin told her where the cinema, churches, good restaurants, and scenic areas were located. She also learned he was a successful developer. He and his girls loved to camp, ski, and go rafting. Jane found herself laughing out loud at Dustin's fishing stories, especially those that included the twins.

When the final whistle blew, signaling the end of the match, the Lady Hawks had seven, the Lady Panthers had three. Cara had two scores, Dara had three. Jared, the mechanic, and his son called to say they would drop off Jane's car at her apartment later that afternoon. All Dustin had to do was take Jane home, but he just couldn't bear to say good-bye—not just yet.

"Jane, I know you just met me and the girls, but I was

wondering if you would like to have lunch with us? We always go to the Burger Barn after a game. It's a family tradition." Dustin chuckled.

Jane thought for a moment. What else did she have to do? Unpack boxes? "Why not?" she said. "I'd love to!"

Dustin was delighted. "Wonderful! The girls will be thrilled to have you come with us."

There was a brief pause. Dustin was as shy as he was handsome, but today Jane Stanley made him throw caution to the wind. "If lunch is a success, Jane, could I persuade you to have dinner with me tonight?" he said softly.

Jane looked into his chiseled face and deep brown eyes, two beautiful little red-headed girls in the background. Nothing had ever felt so *right* before. This wasn't like anything she had expected or planned, but it still felt *right*. Was Dustin Greer just being nice or was he inviting her into his family, into his world? Is the heart *ever* ready when love comes around?

"Lunch would be nice," she answered, unable to keep the smile off her face. "It's not every day a girl is rescued by a good-looking Samaritan."

The Hero

It was a warm, humid Florida morning as the sun rose in the east over The Checkered Flag convenience store. People hurried in and out of the small building, late for work, in a rush to get somewhere. The only stationary person was a man sitting in the shade against the west wall. Nobody gave him half a second's notice. He was just a vagabond, seemingly going nowhere.

The lean homeless man was enjoying a sandwich and juice for breakfast as he watched everyone head toward their destinations. "Destiny," he uttered with a smirk as he watched people going by. "I wish I knew what mine was," he replied sarcastically to himself. He took a huge bite of his ham sandwich and washed it down with a gulp of orange juice. In truth, he had stopped believing in destiny years ago.

The crowd at the corner store diminished as the man finished his meal. He kept his mind entertained by looking at the cars passing by. His daily routine was suddenly interrupted by a violent collision in the middle of the intersection, followed by the loud crunch of grinding steel. A large pick-up had run a red light and side-swiped a small two-door coupe on the driver's side. The little car spun out of control into a lane of oncoming traffic, where a third car, a minivan, brakes fully engaged, slid into the passenger side of the small vehicle. Everyone at the convenience store watched in horror as the dramatic events unfolded and the front of the coupe erupted in flames. The pick-up and minivan drivers got out of their vehicles and ran away from the blazing fire. But the driver of the small auto wouldn't—or couldn't—get out of his vehicle. He was too injured to even cry out for help. He sat in the driver's seat in excruciating pain.

The convenience store manager and several customers watched events unfold through large, tinted windows. "That car is going to explode and kill that man if somebody doesn't do something!" a woman exclaimed. Everyone witnessing the events at the intersection was thinking the same thing, but no one had courage enough to do something about it. Smoke and fire continued to pour out from under the hood like a menacing furnace. The vehicle was sure to explode at any moment.

Suddenly, a man raced toward the flaming inferno.

"Hey, look! Is that Jake?" the store manager said.

The homeless man was headed straight for the driver's window, which was partially open. All eyes were glued to the scene as the scraggly-looking vagabond spoke to the injured driver.

"Are you okay? Can you get out?" the vagabond said to the man.

The wounded man groaned in agony. "I think my left leg is broken," he managed to say. Jake tried to open the driver and passenger doors to help the man out, but they were both severely damaged and wouldn't budge. The driver was trapped in a blazing time bomb that was sure to go off in a matter of seconds!

Jake went back around to the driver's side. "I can't get the door opened!" he exclaimed as smoke and flames continued to pour out from the front of the vehicle like a demonic bonfire.

The man in the car was half conscious now—enough to understand what was happening.

Surrendering to the hopelessness of his situation, the man whispered these words: "My name is Dave—Dave Winkler. I am a police officer. Please tell my wife, Trisha, I love her." Having expended what little strength he had left, the man passed out.

Suddenly Jake was reliving his worst nightmare. He tried again to open the car door, pounding on it frantically. "No! Not again!" he shouted. "This can't be happening again!"

* * * * * * *

The air crackled with the sound of bullets, explosions, and men shouting. The small military unit was under heavy enemy fire as they made their way through the jungle to their extraction point, smoke flares concealing their departure. The *whop whop whop* of helicopter blades could be heard in the distance as they approached the rendezvous site. The soldiers rushed at the two choppers in the clearing as bullets whizzed through the trees. The men climbed into the helicopters as the last member of the team held off the enemy at the tree line with a steady stream of gunfire. As the first helicopter took off safely, Sergeant Jake looked over his left shoulder at the remaining helicopter and knew it was time for him to go. He threw a couple of grenades at the enemy in an effort to buy himself time enough to get on board. He ran to the remaining chopper with all his energy as his friends laid down suppressive fire. An enemy bullet got Jake in the thigh fifteen yards from home. The enemy fire intensified around them and Jake frantically waved for the pilot to leave without him. All of them might get killed if the chopper didn't leave now. "Get out of here while you still can," he shouted to his friends. Jake wasn't afraid of dying. He would gladly fight the enemy to the end, even if he did so alone. He was about to turn and start firing again when one of the men jumped from the safety of the helicopter and came back for him.

He grabbed Jake by the back of his camouflaged uniform and put the wounded man's arm around his own shoulder. They raced to the helicopter while the crew fired a barrage of rounds at the enemy. Jake's savior, his lieutenant, threw the wounded sergeant onto the floor of the helicopter with the help of a few men already inside. Jake remembered lying in the helicopter, watching the lieutenant raise himself to climb in— and then it happened. An enemy bullet struck the lieutenant in the back between his shoulder blades, dropping him next to Jake. The helicopter took off, firing rockets and rounds at the enemy, and headed for the field hospital.

The lieutenant was bleeding heavily from his wound. A medic tried to apply a pressure dressing, but that would not save his life. The lieutenant was dying, and dying fast. Jake was kneeling next to him, encouraging the lieutenant to hang in there, but it wasn't good. The color was quickly draining from his face and his breathing was labored. Jake noticed a bloody necklace with a cross around the man's neck. The lieutenant, with great difficulty, took Jake by the hand. "Jake—you must do something for me," he said. "Tell my wife, Kelly, I love her." Those were lieutenant's last words. He closed his eyes and passed away.

* * * * * * *

Jake was jerked back to the present. "No! Not again!" he shouted. "I can't let *this* officer die like the last one." Something deep inside him cried out to a God he had known before the horrors of war had shaken his faith. "God! Help me, please!" he shouted at the top of his lungs. Just then, he felt the latch to the passenger door give way. Jake wrestled the creaking metal door open and pulled the police officer out. He then literally picked the man up and carried him to the corner store. The flaming car exploded with a mighty *boom* ten seconds later. Jake collapsed to the ground exhausted.

* * * * * * *

The Checkered Flag was a buzz of activity as police, paramedics' and firemen arrived on the scene. Officer Winkler's wife, having rushed to the scene, stood next to her husband as the paramedics stabilized him for transfer to a nearby hospital. When one of the paramedics told her who had rescued her husband, Mrs. Winkler left her husband's side for just a moment and approached Jake, who was standing nearby. "Thank you for saving my husband's life," she told him. Then she gave him an appreciative hug and buried her head in his shoulder in a torrent of emotion. Thanks to Jake she still had her husband and two small children still had their father.

"You're welcome, ma'am," was all Jake could say as she soaked his dirty shirt with grateful tears. Soon after, the ambulance left with siren blasting.

The local news team sent to record the incident and interview witnesses couldn't get enough of Jake, the hero.

"He comes here every morning for breakfast," Mike the store manager told the reporters. He was a fellow veteran and gave Jake a sandwich and juice at the start of each day, which he quietly consumed outside and out of the way. "He's a regular around here," Mike continued. "Very friendly, but quiet.

He likes to keep to himself."

* * * * * * *

Oddly, the motor vehicle accident turned out to be a blessing for Jake. It turned his life around and restored his faith in God. He probably would never fully understand why bad things happen to people. But now he knew that he was loved by his Creator' whose mercy and grace were there for him to help in time of need.[1]

The Winkler family helped Jake get back on his feet. They introduced him to a man in their local church named Joe, who helped the homeless and former prison inmates transition back into mainstream society. Jake was highly gifted in construction work and was soon hired full-time by one of Joe's business contacts. It wasn't long before Jake had his own clothes, apartment, and transportation. He attended church with his newfound Christian friends for Sunday morning services and Wednesday night Bible study. God turned Jake's life around completely. Jake didn't know what God had in store for him next, but one thing was certain. God's thoughts toward him were of peace and not of evil, to give him future and a hope.[2]

* * * * * * *

The first page of the scrapbook had a picture of a little boy and girl playing at the park. Nothing else in the world seemed to matter to them as they drove the dump truck and race car through the winding mountain road they had built in the sand. A delicate hand touched the picture as if trying to hold on to that moment—twenty-eight years ago. What Susan wouldn't give to go back there, just one last time.

She turned the pages slowly, every photo lingering like the fragrance of a walk through a flower garden of memories. There was Susan in her pretty white dress on her seventh birthday with auburn hair, freckles, and blue eyes. As she prepared to blow out the candles, her best friend, Johnny, reminded her to make a wish.

Johnny had always been Susan's best friend. It didn't matter that he was a boy and she was a girl at an age when most boys and girls didn't care for each other. They were an inseparable pair growing up. Their parents were friends, and they shared the same kind of bond.

Susan laughed at the picture of Johnny's ice-cream stained shirt at a high school baseball game. She sighed at their senior prom photos, all dressed up and regal. She smiled at their college graduation picture, the two of them standing together in their gowns. He had earned an accounting degree, while she majored in music.

College graduation was a big deal, not just because they had obtained their degrees but more importantly because they had always thought that would be the time they would marry.

And so…one more milestone fell into place. The wedding was beautiful. She picked up another album and began to move through the exquisite photos. It was all she could have imagined. They had been so happy that first year, so very happy. And then the war began and everything changed quickly. Less than a year after they married, Johnny joined the army.

He sure looked good in that uniform, Susan thought, as she switched albums one more time and turned to his photograph on the last page. Looking at it was always difficult. While she treasured the familiar face, the sadness never failed to overwhelm her. As her delicate porcelain hand reached up and stroked his face, a tear ran down her cheek. Then her eyes moved to the opposite page. The article detailing Johnny's death six years ago still cut like a knife.

> Local Hero Dies in Combat
>
> Captain John Samuel Dexter, age 27, died in combat earlier this week. The tank company commander died during a major battle in enemy-controlled territory in the region of Kadarh. His heroic actions during the fighting saved the lives of many of his men. Memorial services will be held Tuesday at 2:00 p.m. at Bethany Family Church. He is survived by his wife Susan.

Survived is right, thought Susan, as warm tears streamed down her face. They had planned to start a family, raise their children, and grow old together. Life just wasn't the same anymore. How could it be, with Johnny gone? God's love and grace helped her through it all. He gave her the strength to go on.

Susan tried, but there was no room for another man in her heart. Johnny was the only one she had ever known, the only one she ever wanted to know. And now he was gone from this earth. Susan knew it was time to move on. Six years was a long time—too long. But it was all still so painful. After returning the albums to their places in a corner of her bedroom closet, Susan knelt at the foot of her bed and prayed through silent tears, "Lord, I know I need to go forward now. I release Johnny to you. My life is in Your hands. Your will be done."

I love you, My child came the words like water to a thirsty soul. Susan could feel the Lord's presence permeate her being. The words settled over her heart like a warm mist. She remained there for several moments basking in the glory of His presence, a child of God comforted by her heavenly Father. Susan raised herself to her feet with peaceful resignation. She walked to her bathroom mirror and touched up her make-up. Then she brushed her long auburn hair and straightened her flowing blue silk dress. She picked up her Bible and walked out her front door for the Sunday morning service at Bethany Family Church.

* * * * * * *

People trickled into the church building for the service that would soon begin. An elderly lady was escorted out of her vehicle at the main entrance. Parents were taking their little ones to children's church. Others browsed through the bookstore. Susan was greeted at the entrance to the sanctuary and handed a bulletin. As she scanned the auditorium for a place to sit, she saw a woman with long brown hair waving at her. It was her good friend, Trisha Winkler. Susan joined her friend in the fourth row of pews, where they greeted one another joyfully. The two men seated next to Trisha stood up for the introductions.

"Susan, you remember my husband, Dave," Trisha said.

"Yes, of course. Good morning," Susan said to the police officer. Dave greeted her in kind, while Trisha continued with the introductions.

"Susan, we would like you to meet Jake. He is the man who saved Dave's life last year when he had that terrible car accident."

"Oh yes, I have heard so much about you! You're a true hero," Susan gushed. She looked at the lean, muscular, tanned man standing before her. His dark black hair and deep chocolate eyes looked into hers with a serene smile.

"Jake, this is our friend, Susan Dexter," Trisha said somewhere in the background.

"Very nice to meet you, Ms. Dexter," he responded, his strong, confident words washing over her. His handshake was equally strong and warm. "John Samuel Owens, at your service, ma'am."

Susan look stunned. "What did you say your name was?" she asked incredulously. Jake looked a little confused, and glanced at Dave and Trisha. "My name is John—John Samuel Owens," he replied. Dave and Tiffany had not made the connection until that very moment. It was their turn to be surprised.

Susan and John Samuel Owens looked into each other's eyes for several seconds as they shook hands. He felt he was holding the hand of an angel, captivated by the ocean-blue eyes of the beautiful lady standing before him. He tried to suppress the feelings that were quickly rising to the surface.

"Nice to meet you, John Samuel," Susan said softly, her voice faltering at the end. Dave and Trisha looked at each other in a silent exchange. They suddenly felt like intruders in something out of the ordinary.

The service began as the four of them took their seats. Susan sat by the aisle, next to Trisha and Dave Winkler, then John. She glanced over at this new John Samuel, the hero, trying to comprehend what God was doing.

What are you up to, Lord? she thought to herself. Was this merely a remarkable coincidence or the writing on the wall God-style? Her mind was a whirlwind of emotions. Susan didn't know what to think. She dared not think too much. She faced forward to listen to the message and hear what God had to say next.

[1] Hebrews 4:16
[2] Jeremiah 29:11

The Homecoming

Jesse lay in his ICU bed waiting for the end to come. He had signed the DNR (Do Not Resuscitate) order days ago when he was admitted to the hospital with a severe case of pneumonia. Visiting hours were over and his family had gone home for the night. They thought he was going to recover. He knew better. He could feel life ebbing away as he waited. He was ready to go home and be with the Lord. This was a joyful time for him.

The eighty-year-old soldier of God looked back at his service career. He accepted Christ as a teenager at summer camp. His greatest pursuit was a life of service. He volunteered at the shelter in his hometown. He helped feed the poor at the local food pantry. The Lord was getting Jesse ready for a work He had prepared beforehand that he should walk in.[1]

He met Ruth, the daughter of missionary parents, at college. She had missions in her DNA. She quickly realized that missions were part of Jesse's DNA as well. They were married in the campus chapel, always knowing that they were headed to some faraway land as Christ's ambassadors. It was something they talked about constantly.

The homeless and hungry were always in Jesse's thoughts, so much so that they kept him up at night. He lay there remembering a picture he had seen in a magazine of children living in the underground sewers of South America. He could see their tattered clothes, frail bodies, and sunken eyes pleading with him, saying, "Come over and help us."[2]

As soon as possible Jesse and Ruth sold everything and moved to South America. They opened an orphanage and started pulling the children out of the sewers. They rescued hundreds of boys and girls from The Drain, as it was called. Some of them became teachers, social workers, lawyers, and doctors. They all grew up to have families and children of their own, raised in a loving environment.

Jesse and Ruth left The Samaritan's Home in good hands, and returned home after forty years. They had not been able to have children of their own, but that had never mattered. The Lord had entrusted them with hundreds of boys and girls who needed loving parents. They had fulfilled their assignment. They had not been disobedient to the heavenly vision.[3]

After returning to Jesse's hometown, the couple engaged themselves in the shelter and food pantry as if they had never left. Jesse's extended family looked after the two. But then Ruth had passed away in her sleep, and six months later, Jesse had been brought down by pneumonia.

Thoughts of his late wife brought Jesse back to the present moment. He looked around at the flimsy hospital gown he was wearing, the IV in his arm, and the cardiac monitors on his chest. He reached up and touched the oxygen prongs in his nose. His skin was gray and clammy. A faint smile was on face as he contemplated his threshold into eternity with joyful expectation. As his mind and body began to shut down, he whispered, "Lord, I hope you are pleased."

Jesse woke up in his glorified body, standing on a cloud the size of a prairie and feeling young and alive! He was wearing a long, white robe. "Where do I go from here? What now?" he said to himself.

Suddenly, Jesse heard the sound of thunder. He could feel the firmament shaking under his feet and a mysterious power in the air. It was then that they came into his view— approaching armies, riding majestic horses. Their Captain was riding a white horse, and his eyes were like a flame of fire. His robe looked as if it had been dipped in blood and on his robe and thigh were the words KING OF KINGS AND LORD OF LORDS.[4] They were headed his way, and Jesse's heart was racing with excitement.

The great armies came to a halt in front of Jesse. He could see Ruth on one of the steeds, looking radiant. She smiled at him, an extra horse by her side. There was a brief pause. The Lord dismounted from His horse, light shining through nail-pierced hands as He let go of the reins. He began walking toward Jesse.

Every part of Jesse wanted to throw himself at his Lord's feet and worship Him, but somehow he knew he was to remain standing. The Great Commander placed His right hand on Jesse's shoulder, and with a voice of many waters, and the armies of heaven behind Him, He looked into Jesse's eyes and said, "Well done!"[5]

[1] Ephesians 2:10

[2] Acts 16:9–10

[3] Acts 26:19

[4] Revelation 19:11–14, 16

[5] Matthew 25:23

The Interrogation

Phillip's suitcase rested on his bed as he methodically went through his packing list. This was his first trip to the region of Gazahstan and he wasn't sure what to expect. All he knew was the Lord spoke to him to go there on a short-term mission trip. He knew when God says "Go," you go. He went down his checklist one last time.

Bible? Check.

Passport? Check.

Slacks? Check

Shirts? Check.

Shoes? Check.

Sunscreen? Check.

Shades? Check.

Money? Check.

The packing list was complete, or so he thought. Phillip closed his suitcase ahead of schedule, at 6:45 in the morning. His wife, Julie, joined him in their room. "Here, honey," she said, handing him a gift for the local pastor and his wife. He smiled. She always thought about the little things that meant so much. He loved that about her.

"Thank you, darling," he replied. He knew what was coming next, and waited patiently for the moment.

"Phillip, are you sure you are still supposed to go on this trip?"

Gazahstan could be a rough place. Christians had been ill-treated in parts of the country. There were isolated reports of believers being severely persecuted. Julie loved her husband greatly. Even so, she would not allow her emotions to interfere with God's plan. She just needed one last reassurance. Phillip was not annoyed by her questioning. He was glad she cared.

"Yes, Julie. I'm convinced that God wants me to go. The Lord spoke to me clearly, saying, 'Arise and go along the road that goes to Gazahstan.' I don't know why I'm going. All I know is that it's something I'm supposed to do."[1]

They had a quiet breakfast, read the Bible, and prayed together. They talked about the things they would do when he got back. Phillip looked over at Julie as she drove him to the airport and whispered a prayer of thanks to God for the precious wife he had been blessed with. After unloading his bags at the terminal, the couple embraced one last time. Phillip knew it would have to last him until he came home. One hour later, Phillip was on a 747 headed halfway around the world.

As the plane made its climb, Phillip looked down. *Somewhere down there is the woman I love,* he thought. He trusted that he would be coming home to her—because he knew his life was in God's hands. But he couldn't help wondering what would happen if he didn't. After all, not everyone who goes on a mission for the Lord comes back, just as not every soldier who goes to war comes back. It was merely a fact. He didn't feel he was being cynical or fearful.

He had already found out that some people thought such a trip was foolish. A lost world would think it nonsense to go to a nation to which you have never been, at the instruction of a God you cannot see, for a purpose you do not know. Phillip didn't care what the world thought about his obedience to God. "My eyes are on You, Lord," Phillip whispered as he began to doze off to sleep.[2] "Some people on this plane trust a pilot they have never met with their lives more than they trust You. I trust the Lord of the universe with my life more than a total stranger. That's what a sane person would do."

I am glad you see it that way, Phillip, he heard the Lord whisper as he went off to sleep.

Phillip arrived in Gazahstan twenty-eight hours later with a smile on his face. He never complained about long trips. The Apostle Paul would have loved to travel around the world in less than two days. *It's all a matter of perspective,* he reminded himself. He picked up his suitcase at Baggage Claim and made it through Customs without much trouble. It was obvious from his appearance that he was from another part of the world. The officer at Immigration, his last stop, surveyed his passport carefully.

"Why are you here in Gazahstan, Mr. Roberts?" she asked, eyeing him carefully. Her English was excellent. Phillip sensed she had a Western education. He did not perceive any danger here, but he chose his words carefully nonetheless.

"You have a beautiful country, Miss. I have heard many nice things about Gazahstan, and I have come to see if they are all true." His answer changed the atmosphere. Miss Dilahna, as her badge identified her, let him through without further ado, wishing him well on his visit. A soft answer turns away wrath.[3]

Pastors Giorgie and Asha greeted Phillip outside the terminal. They got into the blue compact and took off toward the city. They got to know each other as they made their way to his hotel through winding streets and bustling traffic. Giorgie drove while Phillip rode in the passenger seat.

"We are excited about you coming here, Phillip. Our home church and Bible school students are excited about what you will be sharing with us for the next two weeks. We believe this will be a very good time for everyone. We are so encouraged to have someone come all the way from America to help our ministry."

Phillip was honored by their hospitality. "Thank you, Giorgie and Asha. I am honored to be here. I am thankful the Lord told me to come. I look forward to the time together with the other believers in your church family."

The drive to the hotel seemed like nothing since the three were so busy getting acquainted. While Giorgie and Asha waited in the lobby, Phillip checked in and dropped off his luggage in his room. Then they were off to a popular restaurant in town for more fellowship. They had the time of their lives, eating, talking, and laughing. Food and fellowship with people of like faith and passion is a precious thing, and Phillip loved every minute of it. He handed them the gift from Julie, which they thankfully accepted.

Phillip got back to his hotel room around 10:00 p.m., ready to turn in. He knelt down to pray at the end of his first day in Gazahstan. "Lord, thank You for bringing me here safely. I ask You to protect Giorgie, Asha, and their church family. Let the words of my mouth and the meditation of my heart be acceptable in Your sight during my time here.[4] Your will be done. In Jesus's name, amen." Phillip turned out the bedside lamp and rested his head on the pillow.

The next few weeks flew by as Phillip taught in the church and Bible school. The people were polite and hungry for the Word of God. This local body of believers was being established and encouraged concerning their faith.[5] This time of impartation was changing lives for eternity. The gifts of the Holy Spirit were in operation during many of the meetings. Disciples were being trained and equipped for the work of the ministry.[6]

Giorgie dropped Phillip off by the hotel one afternoon after he was through teaching for the day. His friend sped off as Phillip walked the last fifty yards to the hotel, never suspecting that his friend and brother in the Lord would not make it to the building entrance. Before Phillip had covered half the distance to the front door, a man walked up behind him and put a gun to his back. A huge Mercedes-Benz pulled up to the curb, and he was ordered to get into the backseat. Three men were in the vehicle waiting for him, two in the front and one opposite Phillip in the back.

This is like something from a spy movie, Phillip thought to himself. His mind was racing. *Why is this happening? Anyone who can afford a car like this doesn't need my money.* It made no sense.

Phillip perceived he was not supposed to resist his captors. *Be still, Phillip. Everything is going to be fine?*, he believed God was telling him. The man who put the pistol to Phillip's back got in the car and sat next to him. They put a black hood over his head and handcuffed him as the vehicle drove south into the desert.

For an hour, Phillip and his captors drove in silence. *What would anyone want with me*, Phillip kept asking himself. Then his thoughts turned toward Giorgie, Asha, and the church. *Are they also in danger?* he wondered. And what about Julie and their children, James and Tabitha? *Will I ever see my family again?* That was all that mattered to him at that moment. Phillip began to pray softly.

The Mercedes slowed down and then stopped suddenly. Everyone got out of the car. The sun had gone down and Phillip could feel the desert breeze. He was escorted up some steps toward a building. The air conditioning inside was refreshing. He could tell they were walking on marble floors.

What was this place? Why was he here? The mystery continued. "Lord, I am trusting You," he whispered, not able to see where he was going. Phillip heard large double doors open in front of him, and he was escorted through. Two men, each holding one of his arms, came to a halt. *This is it,* Phillip thought. Once the men removed his handcuffs and hood, Phillip could hardly believe what he was seeing.

"Good evening, Mr. Roberts. Welcome to my home," said a man at the far end of a banquet table. The dining hall was exquisitely decorated with curtains, chandeliers, tapestries, paintings, fountains, and other fine items. There were candles everywhere. Some twenty adults—men and women—were seated at the table. A massive feast was sitting before them. Phillip stood at the other end of the table, standing next to the only empty chair. He was wondering if he should say or do something when the man spoke. "Please sit down, Mr. Roberts," the man smiled. "You are the guest of honor. Let's eat before the food gets cold. Then we will talk."

Phillip sat down as instructed and looked around at his hosts. Those who looked in his direction smiled. The plates, silverware, and glasses were the finest quality. No expense had been spared. He served himself from entrees set before him. A couple sitting next to him encouraged him to try the marinated duck. He was glad he did. Phillip could not remember having eaten such an exquisite meal before. A full stomach is often followed by a merry heart. Phillip decided he would enjoy the moment and try to put aside the fact that he had literally been kidnapped.

Once the meal was finished and the servants had cleared away the dessert trays, Phillip looked in the direction of the man who had welcomed him earlier. He smiled at Phillip and the rest of the people seated with him. Everyone knew to be silent as the master of the house spoke.

"Mr. Roberts, we would like to thank you for joining us for dinner this evening."

I didn't really have a choice, Phillip thought to himself. He looked at his host once again and felt that he was being sincere.

"I apologize for bringing you here in secrecy. I do not want the people of my country to know you were here tonight. My name is Famhir, and this is my beautiful wife, Candace." He held the hand of an elegantly dressed woman seated to his right. She smiled at him and gently bowed her head. Phillip knew to do the same in return. Mr. Famhir continued. "I am a very wealthy and influential man in this country and this part of the world. I would ask that our conversation remain confidential."

"Of course," Phillip answered, still without knowing what this unusual occasion was all about.

"We would like to ask you some questions about this Jesus," Mr. Famhir said.

Phillip could not have been more surprised, but he tried to answer calmly.

"What would you like to know?" he replied.

"Who is He?" Famhir asked.

Phillip paused only for a moment and then he said, "Jesus is the Son of God who came to pay the price for our sins so we could have everlasting life with Him."[7]

"How do you know He is the true God?" Mr. Famhir asked.

Phillip answered without hesitation this time. "Since the creation of the world His invisible attributes are clearly seen, being understood by things that are made, even His eternal power and Godhead.[8] All men know there is a God. We know Him through His inspired book, the Bible. When you read His Word, you will know in your heart that He is the one true God."

"What is He like?" asked Candace.

"Oh, He is wonderful—like no other. He is patient and kind. He does not envy, nor does He parade Himself around. He is not puffed up. He does not behave rudely, seek His own selfish interests, and He is not easily provoked. He does not rejoice in iniquity, but in the truth. He bears all things, believes all things, hopes all things, and endures all things. He is love, and love never fails."[9]

An elderly man a couple of seats away was reading a Bible. He looked at Phillip and asked, "What does it mean to be born again?"

"It means to be spiritually alive when you accept Jesus as your Lord and Savior. The Spirit of God Himself comes to live inside of you and you are born again, this time of the Spirit."[10]

The elderly man looked down and started pounding his chest with his hand. "You mean the Spirit of God comes inside me?" he said. "I can hardly believe God would do this."

Phillip smiled. "It is difficult to believe, and yet It is true. We become a new creation.[11] God wants to have a relationship with each of us, for we are His own creation."

There was silence in the dining hall as Phillip's words began to sink into the hearts of those around the table.

Mr. Famhir spoke again. "Mr. Roberts, we would all like to become Christians and meet Jesus. We would like to have the Spirit of God in our hearts. What must we do?"

Phillip responded once again without hesitation. "If you confess with your mouth the Lord Jesus and believe in your heart that God has raised Him from the dead, you will be saved.[12] Can we hold hands and pray?" Everyone agreed excitedly, holding hands with eyes closed.

Phillip prayed in English while Famhir translated for those who did not speak English. "Lord Jesus, thank You for dying on the cross for my sins. I know You love me and have forgiven me. I ask You to be the Lord of my life and come live in my heart. I will obey Your Word and live the rest of my life for You. Amen."

Everyone got up from the table, excited about their new life with the one true God. Mr. Famhir and Candace walked up to Phillip and invited him for a walk on their estate. Everyone else followed behind them. As they walked down some steps, they came to a large pool and garden.

"I see there is water," Phillip said. "The next step is for all of you to be baptized, dipped in the water, as a sign of your new life in Christ." They all went down into the water and he baptized them all. It was the best pool party he ever attended!

Everyone gave Phillip a hug when it was time to take him back to his hotel room. Famhir and Candace were left alone with their guest. "Phillip, we would like to thank you for being here today and sharing Jesus with us," he began. Famhir signaled for one of his servants to approach them. He held out a small, wooden box and opened it for his master. Inside the box was a gold ring with an elephant engraved on it, a diamond in its eye.

Famhir took the ring and placed it on Phillip's right index finger. "This is the symbol of my family," he said. "As long as you wear this ring, no one can touch you while you are in Gazahstan."

Candace also had a small jewelry box for Julie, which Phillip received joyfully. "Thank you both for an evening I will never forget," he said. "I do not know when I will ever come back to Gazahstan, but this trip has been one of the greatest experiences of my life."

Candace spoke up. "We were hoping you and your wife could come stay with us for a week in a few months' time. We need to learn more about Jesus."

Phillip knew it would be a financial stretch to do as they requested, but he knew God would provide. "We would be delighted to return in two months," he said.

"Good. My secretary will contact you when you get home. She will take care of the travel arrangements for you to fly in my personal jet." They all gave each other a customary hug and Phillip got back in the car with the driver. Famhir and Candace waved to him as they drove away.

Julie isn't going to believe this, he thought to himself.

Phillip waited for Julie outside the international terminal in Houston. She honked at him as she pulled up to the curb. He didn't recognize the car she was driving. They owned a Mazda but this wasn't it. Julie got out of the car excitedly and hugged him. They put his suitcase in the back of the car and drove off. Julie had so much to say.

"Honey, you won't believe this! I got a call from the Mazda dealership. We won a promotional free car from a list of previous Mazda owners. All I had to do was turn in our old model for this brand-new one!"

"That's great," Phillip said. Then he looked down at the key ring that came with the car. It had an elephant engraved on it with a diamond in its eye, Phillip smiled.

They were soon pulling into their driveway, only ten short minutes from the airport. After bringing in his bags from the car, Phillip sat down at his library desk. While Julie prepared something to eat in the kitchen, he went through the mail. A letter from the mortgage company caught his eye. He opened the envelope and read a brief note.

Dear Mr. Roberts,

We are glad to inform you that the remaining balance on your mortgage has been paid in full. It has been a pleasure doing business with you.

Sincerely,

Michael Reynolds

Mr. Mike Reynolds
Chairman, Loan Services

Now it was Phillip's turn to be excited. He read the letter several times, and then finished going through the mail. Soon he came across an envelope addressed to him from Central Christian University. Their daughter Tabitha was starting school there in the fall. It was going to take everything they had to pay for her education. He opened the envelope and found a letter from the president of the university.

Dear Mr. Roberts,

It is a pleasure for me to write you personally. A benefactor has paid for Tabitha to attend CCU free of charge for her Bachelor's and Master's degrees. We look forward to seeing her on campus in a few months.

In His name,

Elizabeth Stein

Dr. Elizabeth Stein
President, CCU

Phillip was completely astounded! He didn't know what to say or do. All he knew was to rejoice! He leaned back in his chair, put his arms in the air, and started praising God, warm tears running down his face. Julie walked in on him with soup and cheese sandwiches, a curious look on her face. She set dinner on his desk and got cozy in a leather chair by a table lamp.

"So, honey, tell me about your trip," she said, taking a big bite of her cheese sandwich. Phillip looked at her affectionately, a smile on his face. He pulled the jewelry box Candace gave him out of his coat pocket and looked inside. He decided to wait until Julie finished eating before showing her the huge, black pearl necklace.

"Get comfortable, Julie. This is going to take awhile," Phillip laughed.

[1] Acts 8:26

[3] Proverbs 15:1

[4] Psalm 19:14

[5] 1 Thessalonians 3:1–2

[6] Ephesians 4:11–12

[7] John 3:16

[8] Romans 1:20

[9] 1 Corinthians 13:4–8

[10] John 3:6

[11] 2 Corinthians 5:17

[12] Romans 10:9

The Invitation

It was winter in Vermont and the Townsends were excitedly planning their annual golf tournament vacation. Denise was at the kitchen table laptop making flight reservations. Vernon was on his cell phone with the Turtle Bay Resort in beautiful Hawaii. The couple had become avid golfers after their children left the nest to go to college. Jenny and Trent were certain their parents' passion for the game would wear off eventually, but so far that hadn't happened. This was the couple's fourth consecutive year spending a week in the Aloha State for The Turtle Bay Ladies Invitational.

Trent read the latest issue of *Explorer* magazine in the den while his parents eagerly planned their next trip. He hoped they wouldn't try again to drag him halfway around the world to watch another *meaningless* golf tournament. He was a wild wilderness kind of guy who had no use for a goofy golf course. His hopes were dashed when his mother spoke up. He listened quietly to her dissertation on why he should go.

"Trent, *darling*," his mother started, "you *must* come with us this year. We know you will have a wonderful time. Some of the best female golfers in the world are going to be at the tournament. There will be a lot to do and see—the beach, ocean, recreational activities, and luaus. I know you would have the time of your life!" There was a brief pause. "Who knows? Maybe you will even meet a pretty girl," she concluded playfully.

Trent took a deep breath, lowered his magazine, and faced Denise. "Mother, I don't need to fly halfway across the globe to meet a pretty girl. You two know I don't like golf. I would much rather be on a boat in the middle of the Amazon jungle than a fancy golf resort in Hawaii. You want to talk about beauty. Now *that's* beauty," he finished, thinking the debate was over. Trent felt a pinprick of conviction when he saw his mother sighing, her hopes dashed. Vernon got off the phone to participate in the discussion. His dad looked him in the eyes with that scolding look parents master over the years. Trent knew he was in trouble.

"You promised to go with us last year and backed out at the last minute." There was a prolonged silence. Trent had nowhere to hide. Dad was right. He freely agreed to go last year and then came up with a lame excuse about having to study over winter break. He had hurt his mother's feelings in the process. No matter how little he cared for golf, Trent realized he needed to make things right.

"You're right, Dad. I'm sorry about last year, mom. I'll go with you," he said.

* * * * * * *

Trent stood on the edge of the eighteenth fairway on the last day of the Turtle Bay Invitational. The fourth and last day of the event had slowly, but mercifully, come to an end. Trent had occupied a good portion of his time running on the beach, swimming, and horseback riding when not on the golf course with his parents. Denise and Vernon looked on as the last group was about to tee off. Trent watched exotic birds in the trees, oblivious to what was happening around him. Die-hard golf fans were scattered along both sides of the fairway, with a huge crowd around the eighteenth green. Mom and dad were nearby, somewhere, as he looked up in the trees at a warbler.

Just then, Trent heard some commotion around him and people moving. And finally, a *thump* accompanied by a pain on the side of his head. Everything went dark.

* * * * * * *

The tournament temporarily came to a halt, all eyes fixed on Trent lying on the ground. Paramedics took him away to the nearest emergency room as his parents looked on with concern. Dr. Mark Komi had been watching the whole thing live on television. As the medical doctor on call, he was contacted by the ER staff to take a look at Trent. Blood tests and a CT scan of the head were negative, but Trent still had a headache, some dizziness, and nausea. He sat in his community hospital bed, hooked up to an IV in disbelief.

Dr. Komi decided to keep Trent overnight for observation. The Turtle Bay Resort would want to avoid bad publicity or a lawsuit. Their insurance policy covered all the expenses. From his hospital bed, Trent saw himself sprawled out on the ground on the local evening news. He also gazed at the mango and palm trees outside his window. But the sun had gone down a couple of hours ago, and he was getting bored.

Just then someone knocked at the door.

"Come in," Trent said, thinking it must be yet another hospital tech coming to check his vitals. He couldn't have been more wrong!

As Trent stared, one of the most beautiful creatures he had ever seen walked into the room. The lovely young woman looked to be in her twenties. She had short blond hair and was wearing white shorts, leather sandals, and a lovely red blouse. This unexpected beauty had a perfect tan and a pearly smile. Her aqua-blue eyes were mesmerizing. She had Trent's complete and absolute attention.

"Excuse me. Are you Trent Townsend?" she asked shyly.

For an instant, Trent thought he was dreaming. The headache and dizziness were gone. He wanted to pull out his IV and take her in his arms just to see if she was real. Deep down, he knew she *was* real and managed to restrain himself.

"Yes. Yes I am," he said excitedly. She smiled again and stepped a little closer to the bed.

"My name is Stacy Merchant. It was my golf ball that hit you on the head. I came to check on you and make sure that you're going to be okay," she said, with the voice of an angel.

"Yes, I'm fine. A little bump on the head, that's all. The doctor wanted me to stay overnight just to be safe. I'm supposed to get out of here in the morning," Trent answered.

"I'm so glad you're doing better," she replied. "My plane leaves in the morning. I wanted to come by for a moment and check on you before leaving."

Trent's mind was churning. Her last words spun in his thoughts as if in a blender. *Before leaving. Before leaving* for far away. *Before leaving* for the rest of my life. *Before leaving* forever. He had to do something. He spoke up in a moment of unparalleled boldness.

"Excuse me, Stacy. I know you are supposed to leave in the morning, but would you be willing to stay another day? Maybe have lunch with me and my parents?" He knew the chances of her saying yes were one in a million, but he couldn't live with himself if he didn't ask her.

"It is really nice of you to ask. I already have plans to leave tomorrow though." Trent didn't blame her for being unwilling to change her itinerary for a total stranger. His hopes started to dwindle, but boldness rose up in him again, unwilling to take no for an answer.

"Please stay another day. My mom and dad are huge golf fans. They would love to meet you. Besides, the way I see it, you owe me one," he said with a wry smile. That got her attention.

"What makes you say *that*?" she asked quizzically.

"Several reasons," he replied, with growing confidence. "First, my mom told me your ball was going into the trees and would have cost you the lead. By bouncing off my head and back into the fairway, you were able to save par and win the tournament. Second, if the ball had come a few inches closer and hit me in my temple it could have killed me. As it is, I have had to spend a night here at the hospital. The *least* you could do is spend an extra night at Turtle Bay." *Third*, Trent thought to himself, *you are the most beautiful girl I've ever met and I can't stand the thought of not ever seeing you again.*

Stacy raised an eyebrow and smiled. "You're not trying to guilt trip me, are you?"

"If that's what I have to do to get you to stay another day, yes I am," he replied, half-joking, half-desperate.

Stacy looked into Trent's deep brown eyes. Her resolve diminished the longer their conversation continued. Her heart warmed to his good humor and friendly smile. Was his invitation fate or insanity? She didn't know. She looked into those brown eyes again.

"I guess I can stay over one more day. It will be nice to have a little rest before the long flight back to the mainland," she replied with a smile and a small spark in her eyes.

* * * * * * *

Trent's parents arrived bright and early the next morning to take him back to the hotel. He met them with a cheery smile and a bounce in his step.

"By the way," he started, "I've invited a girl named Stacy Merchant to join us for lunch today."

Denise laughed loudly. "That's very funny, dear," she replied, holding her side.

Vernon looked at him and chuckled. "You *really* did get hit hard by that golf ball, didn't you?" he chimed in.

"*I'm serious,*" Trent continued. It took quite awhile, but he was finally able to persuade his parents that he *was* telling them the truth. He shared the events at the hospital from the night before. The transformation in Denise and Vernon was amazing. They went from laughter and disbelief to utter excitement and anticipation. Stacy Merchant, the second-ranked ladies' golf player in the world, was having lunch with them today! This was their best vacation trip ever.

The three of them were sitting at a resort restaurant table when Stacy walked in. She spotted Trent, smiled shyly, and joined them. It turned out to be quite a lunch. The four of them joked, laughed, and told stories like they had been best friends for many years. Several hours later, Denise and Vernon left Trent and Stacy in the restaurant to enjoy dessert. Denise gave Stacy a warm hug before leaving.

"Your parents are really nice," she remarked, watching them head back to the elevators.

"Yes they are. They love golf. Meeting you was the highlight of their trip." There was a brief pause as he looked into her eyes. "Mine too," he added. Stacy could feel herself feeling warm all over. The sensation delighted her.

"My parents and I have a couple more days here before going back to Vermont. I was hoping you could stay a few more days. We would be glad to pay for your room."

Stacy felt warm all over again. She looked into Trent's brown eyes. Fate or insanity? She looked into his brown eyes again and knew the answer better than she knew herself.

"I would love to stay," she replied, smiling, eyes moist. "It is very kind of you to offer, but you won't need to pay for my room. The owner of the resort is a friend of mine. She will be glad to let me stay a few extra days and mingle with the guests. What shall we do next?" She asked with a playful smile.

* * * * * * *

Trent and Stacy sat on recliner chairs on the beach by the water at Turtle Bay. A full moon watched them sipping pineapple tea. The Turtle Bay Ladies Invitational championship trophy rested on the sand between them. Gentle waves could be heard making it to shore.

"To think I didn't want to come on this vacation trip," he said. "Look at what I would have missed out on." He reached for her hand and turned to gaze into her eyes. Stacy laughed softly, taking another sip of her pineapple tea.

"I am glad you came, too," she responded. There was a pause. "I could use a new caddie," she announced playfully.

Trent pondered her words for a few seconds. "I'll make you a deal, Stacy Merchant. I'll be your caddie if you will come with me on a tour of the Amazon River.

"How can a girl turn down an invitation like that," she said playfully.

They both laughed.

The Last Request

The Maxwell Law Firm in Stony Cove, Oregon, had been helping people for three generations. Ethan was proud to be part of it. But now sitting at his desk fulfilling his last obligation to a longtime friend, he couldn't help but feel sad. As executor of Randy Jennings's will, he was looking at two letters written by his deceased friend. He paused for a moment and looked up at several framed photographs on his wall. He and Randy were standing next to each other in their high school football team picture. A few inches away, there was another more recent photo of Randy wearing his camouflage uniform. The smile on his face showed that he was happy to be serving his country even in that hot, desert environment. But sadly, the young major hadn't made it home. His funeral service had taken place at the Jennings's local church a month earlier.

Randy had prepared well for the possibility of his death during military service. His wife, Tanya, was the sole beneficiary of his two life insurance policies, allowing her to pay off the mortgage on their coastal home outside of town and to start a printing business as an investment for the future. All personal assets had been transferred to Randy's widow. Only one piece of business remained. Randy had left two letters in Ethan's possession to be mailed after his funeral.

One of the letters was addressed to Tanya. No problem

there. But the second letter was addressed to someone Ethan had never met—a Mr. Perkins in Arizona. Ethan wasn't quite sure what that letter was all about, but he was eager to fulfill his friend's instructions. He took the letters to the post office and sent them by certified mail to their destinations.

* * * * * * *

Tanya came home late from work that evening. She was surprised when the doorbell rang and the postman asked her to sign for a certified letter from The Maxwell Law Firm. After following the postman's instructions, she made herself comfortable in her chair in the den, tore open the letter with shaking hands, and began to read her husband's last words to her.

> *My Beloved Tanya,*
>
> *If you are reading this letter, then I have passed away in the service of our beloved country. Freedom comes at a price and we agreed to pay that price, however much, when we became a military family.*
>
> *You have been a better wife than I could have ever have asked, dreamed of, or prayed for. I cherished every moment we spent together. You invaded my life with your love and I had no choice but to completely surrender to you. I know you are grieving my loss right now, but there will be a time to love and laugh again. Your physical and emotional needs are of the utmost concern to me. I promised I would always take care of you, and I am saying the following with that in mind.*
>
> *I would like to ask you to find room in your*

heart for someone else after I am gone. Someone who will love and care for you as I did. There is only one person I feel I can trust with your care. His name is Ben Perkins, my good friend from my early years in the military. Being in combat together caused us to form a strong bond. He is like a brother to me. He left the military several years ago and now teaches history at a university in Arizona. His wife died of cancer shortly before his military commitment was completed. I have never seen a man more devoted to his wife. He has not remarried and lives alone.

I am asking you to meet with him for lunch at your house exactly four months after receipt of this letter. I have also written to him with the same instructions. He will be there.

My last request is that the two of you meet to discuss the possibility of marriage. He is an honorable man and will love and care for you. He needs you as much as you need him. What the two of you decide after you meet is a decision you must make on your own.

With all my love,
Randy

P.S. I have enclosed a picture of Ben. His favorite food is lasagna.

Tanya folded the letter and placed it on the night table. She buried her head in her hands and started sobbing.

* * * * * * *

Professor Ben Perkins was relaxing in his library when the doorbell rang. The postman showed him where to sign for the certified letter from The Maxwell Law Firm in Stony Cove, Oregon. He had been in Stony Cove just last month for his good friend Randy's funeral. It had to be connected to Randy's death, he reasoned, but what it was he couldn't imagine. Upon opening the letter, he found that it was from Randy himself. He sat back down in his chair and began to read.

> *Dear Ben,*
>
> *If you are reading this letter, it means I have been buried and moved on to my heavenly home. You have been a good friend over the years, and in my mind, you embody honor, integrity, and commitment more than anyone I know. I am writing you as a friend and brother.*
>
> *I am asking you to do something for me. I want you to marry Tanya, my widow. You need her and she needs you. She is sure to make you as blissfully happy as she made me during our marriage. I know you will care and provide for her in the same way you did for Caroline.*
>
> *You are to meet Tanya for lunch at her house exactly four months after this letter is received. During that meeting you are to discuss the possibility of marriage. This is my last request. I know you won't disappoint me.*
>
> *Randy*

P.S. I have enclosed a picture of Tanya. Her favorite flowers are pink roses.

The letter fell to the floor after Ben finished reading it. Losing Caroline was hard enough. "Randy, I can't do this again" he whispered.

* * * * * * *

Tanya sat in her living room fidgeting with her hands and looking up at the clock. Twenty-five minutes past eleven in the morning. Was this really happening? Would Ben from Arizona really show up at her door? This all seemed a little insane. Correction, this *was* insane! She pinched herself to make sure she was awake. She was.

She had just looked up at the clock one more time, when she heard a car pull up in the driveway. It was exactly 11:45 a.m. Tanya peeked through the curtains and saw a tall man coming up the wooded walkway to the front of the house. Randy was right. He would be here. *He was here!* The doorbell rang. Tanya stood on the other side of the door in a long white skirt and a soft blue flowing blouse. She took a deep breath, grabbed the door knob, and slowly pulled it open.

She paused long enough to take a good look at the tall, handsome man standing before her. He was wearing jeans, a brown long-sleeve shirt, and chocolate blazer. Ben smiled at her nervously. "You must be Tanya," he said somewhat hesitantly.

"Yes. Yes I am," she replied. They stared at each other for a few seconds. "Please come in!" she said finally.

"Thank you," he replied. Ben surveyed the house as he followed Tanya into the den where a warm fireplace greeted him. The home was exquisitely designed and decorated, a combination of both modern and regional styles. A spacious sun room in the back of the house provided a spectacular view of Stony Cove and the surrounding coastline. "You have a beautiful home here," Ben remarked with genuine admiration.

Tanya smiled. "Thank you. An architect friend designed it for us. This is where I stayed whenever Randy was deployed." It was impossible to avoid mentioning Randy in their conversation. He had been such a big part of both their lives. They talked about Randy for quite a while, exchanging stories and fond memories.

Awhile later, Tanya invited Ben into the den and offered him a cup of hot chocolate, which he gratefully accepted. She made a cup for each of them and then made herself comfortable on the sofa across from him.

"Randy and I were in the same unit early in our careers when I was a first lieutenant," Ben began. "We fought together in Iraq. We both made captain upon returning to the States. I changed units and duty stations, but we continued to communicate periodically. I believe the two of you were married shortly after he returned from the Middle East."

"That's correct," Tanya added. "Randy and I were engaged during his first deployment. We got married several months after he returned. We were high school sweethearts. We had been married four years when his convoy was attacked during his last deployment and he was killed. He only had a couple of weeks left, and I was really looking forward to having him home for good," she concluded, wiping a tear from her eye. A fresh log in the fireplace crackled. There was an awkward silence between them before Ben spoke again.

"Caroline and I were high school sweethearts as well." He produced a picture from his wallet of a pretty woman, slender with light skin, long red hair, and blue eyes. "She died of pancreatic cancer shortly before I got out. I watched her go from a beautiful, athletic ball of energy to a shell of a person in just six months," he said somberly.

"I am so sorry to hear that. You must have loved her very much," Tanya added.

"I did," Ben replied. There was a brief silence before he continued. "I was surprised to receive Randy's letter. I didn't know if I would be able to come here after losing Caroline the way I did." There was another brief pause as Ben looked away through the sun room to the ocean's tumultuous waves. "I must admit, this is a pretty awkward way to meet," he said, "for both of us." He couldn't help thinking how she must be feeling.

"It *is* awkward for me, I won't lie. Randy thought very highly of you, however, and I felt I needed to honor his last request by meeting with you."

"I came for the same reason," Ben paused momentarily. "I thought you might want to hear what Randy wrote me."

Tanya's curiosity perked up a bit. She nodded, wondering what her deceased husband had told his friend. Ben read Tanya the brief, but very personal, note. She became teary eyed at the part about making her husband blissfully happy.

Tanya bowed her head and remained quiet for a moment. She looked up at Ben. "I hope you understand if I don't read the letter he wrote me," she said softly. "Some of the things he said are very personal."

Ben looked at Tanya. The picture Randy had included with the letter didn't do her justice. Her dirty blond hair, oval brown eyes, and prominent cheekbones were strikingly beautiful. Her pendulous bosom and slim waist made her even more irresistible. Beyond her obvious physical beauty, Ben saw a hurting, delicate woman. In that moment, he had a sudden urge to take her in his arms and comfort her. She stirred emotions in him he thought had disappeared with Caroline's passing.

Another thought occurred to Ben. Randy knew an intimate meeting between him and Tanya might light a spark between them. If that had been Randy's intent, his plan was proving successful. A spark had been lit and Ben sensed an early flame was beginning to kindle inside him. He was having difficulty seeing clearly from all the smoke the small fire was creating. He heard Tanya's soft voice say something in the distance.

"I apologize for making this meeting so difficult," she confessed.

"There is no need to apologize," Ben responded kindly. *You can't help being so beautiful and irresistible,* Ben thought, wondering how he could be experiencing such a strong physical and emotional attraction to a woman he had just met. He'd been holding onto Caroline's memory for so long— maybe too long. Maybe it was time to let himself have these feelings again.

"Tanya, we both miss Randy and Caroline. There's nothing wrong with that. But they are gone and we are here. I would very much like to get to know you better, if you would allow me to do so." Ben held his breath, waiting for her reply.

Tanya looked into his deep brown eyes. Randy said Ben was an honorable man and that he would love and care for her. Would she be able to reciprocate that love? She wasn't at all sure, but it wouldn't hurt to find out. "I would like that," she said, the first feelings of affection bubbling inside her.

Ben's heart skipped a beat. They had both opened their hearts ever so slightly. Could they let each other in? Only time would tell.

"I'm going to be here for a week. I have colleagues and graduate students covering a couple of my classes, except for those I teach online. Would you take a drive with me along the coast this weekend?"

Tanya smiled softly. "That sounds like fun. Maybe we could stop along the way and have lunch. I know several good places." There was a brief pause before Tanya spoke again. "Ben, there are a couple of things I think you should know before we go any further." She took a deep breath, hesitant to share something so personal with a virtual stranger. But he had a right to know from the beginning. "I'm not able to have children."

Taken a little by surprise, Ben stammered for a few seconds. But he quickly got his bearings and answered her honestly. "I wouldn't ask or expect you to do so." She gave him a smile.

"And there's something else," she continued. "I don't plan to leave Stony Cove. This is my home. All my family is here."

"I understand. I would never ask you to leave," he answered. "You should know that I have a lot of flexibility in my career. I teach most of my classes online, and should I decide to move here, there are several colleges and universities in the area where I could find part-time work. In fact, my family owns a large corporation with a regional office in Seattle. I may be helping oversee operations there from time to time."

Tanya smiled. It all seemed too easy, almost meant to be. It gave her goose bumps. Just then she remembered lunch! "Oh my goodness! It's time to eat! Lunch is in the oven."

Tanya led Ben to the sunroom where a square table was set for two. While Ben enjoyed the view of Stony Cove and the great Pacific ocean, she placed two glasses of water, a salad, and a pan of lasagna on the table.

"What a treat. I love lasagna," Ben told her.

"I know. Randy told me." She laughed.

Once she was seated, Ben asked if he could say grace, and Tanya quickly agreed. He reached out for her hand, but suddenly Tanya seemed uncertain. "Too much too soon, perhaps," he said quietly.

"It's all right," she replied. She looked into Ben's eyes and gave him her hand. There was no *yes* or *I do* spoken but they both understood. The door to her heart was now open once again. He squeezed her hand ever so gently in acknowledgment, both of them with watery eyes.

They had already bowed their heads when Ben abruptly jumped up from the table. "Excuse me, Tanya, but there is something I forgot to do! Please close your eyes. I'll be right back."

She heard Ben go out the front door and then back in again. She kept her eyes closed until she heard him sit down next to her. "You can open your eyes now," he said.

Tanya gasped softly. A glass vase with a dozen pink roses rested on the table. "Randy told you, didn't he?" she said, laughing.

"Yes, he did." Ben smiled. He took her hand this time and didn't let go. They closed their eyes, bowed their heads, and gave thanks.

The Lilies

It was a cold and indifferent February night as Melissa exited the hospital onto the parking lot. She had a great deal on her mind as she walked to her car. Losing your job can do that to you. Decreasing deliveries at the hospital meant fewer newborn nursery admissions. Fewer newborn nursery admissions meant fewer newborn nursery nurses. As the most junior RN on staff, Melissa was the first to go. Finding a new job would take awhile. She did not know many people in town, having just moved from out of state three months earlier. She was just starting to build up her savings as well. The timing for this layoff could not have been worse. All she needed was something else to go wrong.

Melissa got into her Honda and drove across the street to a convenience store. She was low on milk and bread and decided to get some before going home. She parked in the only available parking space, near the side of the building. The lighting was so poor that she didn't see the man with the gun until he was right up on her.

Suddenly realizing her predicament, Melissa froze in her tracks. She gasped for breath as the assailant started yelling at her to hand over her purse. She tried to comply, but she couldn't seem to move, even though she could sense that the gunman was becoming impatient and more irate. Melissa was certain he would shoot her. The gunman pointed the pistol at her, ready to fire. Just then a stranger tackled the gunman and pulled him to the ground. The weapon fired, hitting nothing, as the two wrestled for control of the gun.

Both the men had a hand on the pistol when a second round went off. Melissa's benefactor had been shot in the right thigh. Melissa collapsed to the ground, kneeling behind the brave stranger.

The assailant was in a rage as he got to his feet. He stared at the two of them with cruel, dark eyes as he slowly aimed his pistol at the wounded man's chest and began to pull back on the trigger.

Then suddenly the gunman stopped. He looked past Melissa and the wounded stranger as though petrified. Only he could see the nine-foot-tall angel holding a sword in a battle stance, standing behind the pair. The gunman dropped the pistol and ran.

Melissa was still kneeling next to the wounded man. A puddle of blood had formed around his leg and he looked pale. *He saved my life and I don't even know his name,* she thought, hearing sirens for the first time.

"Are you okay?" he asked with a faint smile.

"Yes," she whispered, tears running down her face.

"Thank God," he replied, and passed out in her arms.

* * * * * * *

Paul woke up the next day in a medical-surgical ward. He had taken care of many patients in this very place, but this time the tables were turned. He was the patient now. His thigh was wrapped with a huge dressing, and an IV was connected to his left hand. *It's amazing how surgery, several units of blood, and some intravenous fluids will make you feel better,* he thought to himself.

Paul came from a long line of doctors. The name Remington was synonymous with community service in Shiloh. The wealthy, down-to-earth family had served the town as physicians for generations. In his early forties, Paul was already semi-retired. He still continued to practice, however, because he loved helping people. He was both an excellent surgeon and a kind person. He never charged people from his local church for his services.

News of Paul's injury was a big deal in Shiloh. He looked around his room and was amazed to see that half of his floor space was taken up by flowers from friends, family, and hospital staff. Wendy, his nurse, regulated the stream of visitors that started pouring in, including physicians and hospital staff. Everyone was glad to see him and thankful he was alive.

A private man who disdained publicity, Paul was dismayed when he saw his story on the front page of the local newspaper. *How am I going to live up to this legend?* he thought to himself.

As his visitors diminished somewhat during the course of the morning, the hospital's chief medical officer dropped by to see him. Paul had nominated him for the job a few years ago. There were days when Dr Stevens, an internist, didn't know whether to thank Paul or be angry at him for the favor.

"Well, Paul, now you've really done it!" his friend said, glancing at the paper laying on the bed. *"Lady at gunpoint rescued by the fearless Dr. Remington,"* he continued. "I can just picture the cards you will get in the mail. 'Dr. Remington, will you be my Valentine?' signed *Damsel in Distress.* What possible chance do the rest of us have?"

Paul had to laugh at his friend's jabs. "Don't be silly, Jim. Besides, who is going to be interested in a wounded duck like me?" Paul had been single for three years since the unexpected death of his wife. During that time, he hadn't even looked at another woman. Some wounds take a long time to heal. There was a brief pause.

"I'm sure one day you'll find the right girl," Steve said before the conversation took a more serious turn. "We all thank God you're alive, Paul." His colleague got up from his chair and moved to the door. "We look forward to having you back in the OR after you're mended," he said, and closed the door behind him.

For the next few moments, Paul reflected on the incident he had so narrowly survived. He thought about the young woman at the store, hoping she had not been badly traumatized. He realized that he hadn't even gotten her name. *Life sure has its twists and turns,* he thought.

Just then there was a knock on the door. "Come in," Paul called out. As the door slowly opened, Paul could see that it was the woman from the store! He recognized her beautiful blue eyes and long brown hair. He motioned to her to come in.

"Welcome to my humble room," he said with a smile. "How are you doing?"

"I'm doing just fine, thanks to you," she answered. "A little shaken up but no worse for wear."

"Terrific," said Paul with a grimace. He was trying to be more hospitable by sitting himself up higher in bed.

Melissa looked concerned. "I should be asking how you're doing," she continued. "I am so sorry this happened to you, Dr. Remington."

"Please, just call me Paul," the doctor said, trying to put her at ease. "I consider myself fortunate. The injury could have been much worse. No bones were broken. I will need to take it easy for the next several months, but that just means I'll be able to spend some extra time with my family. I'm looking forward to that."

Just then a girl and an older woman burst into the room.

"Daddy! Daddy!" the twelve-year-old girl cried out, as she ran to Paul and gave him a big hug.

"Speaking of my family, here they are now," Paul said, wrapping his arms around his only child. "This is my daughter, Lily, and this is my aunt Betty." Paul motioned to a woman standing at the door. They both turned to Melissa and greeted her with a smile and a handshake.

With that, Paul looked into Melissa's eyes. "I'm so sorry," he said. "We've survived a near-death experience together, and we've been talking for a little while now, but I still haven't gotten your name."

Lily and Aunt Betty looked at each other with a curious smile.

"My name is Melissa—Melissa Wright. It's very nice to meet both of you," she said, smiling at Lily and Aunt Betty.

"Melissa, it is so good to meet you. I was told you are one of our pediatric nurses," Paul started.

"*Was* is more like it, Dr. Remington—Paul." Once again, Lily and aunt Betty exchanged smiles. "I had just been told that I was being let go when all this happened," she explained. "I may have to move back to Virginia if I don't find work soon." There was a brief silence, then Paul spoke up.

"Melissa, since it would seem that you are currently unemployed, would you be interested in a job offer? Aunt Betty lives in a bungalow on our estate, and she could use some help around the property. I think she would also enjoy your company. Lily and I normally plant flowers in the springtime. It is one of our favorite family activities. She is going to need someone to help her this year because of my injury. I am also going to need someone who can drive her around. I will gladly provide you with room, board, and your regular salary for three months while you are looking for a new job. That should be plenty of time to help you get back on track."

Melissa was completely surprised by Paul's overture. She stood there, speechless.

Lily chimed in before Melissa could answer. "Yes! Yes! Melissa. Please, come stay with us!"

Then it was Aunt Betty's turn. "I think this is a great idea. We should at least give it a try, don't you think so, dear?"

Melissa was overwhelmed by their generosity and hospitality. "Very well," she said. "I guess it's the least I can do to help after your injury. I accept."

With that the three women said their good-byes and left Paul to rest. He could hear them making plans for Melissa to move in the following week. He began to doze off as fatigue and his pain medication kicked in. The Great Physician was preparing a remedy for his heart condition while he slept.

* * * * * * *

Aunt Betty's place was beautiful. She gave Melissa a tour of her cozy home. The two-bedroom bungalow was perfect for guests. Melissa's face lit up when Aunt Betty showed her the room she would be staying in. She liked the traditional, modern feel of the space.

After dropping off her bags, Melissa joined Betty in the kitchen. They were soon getting acquainted while peeling potatoes. Melissa admired the kitchen as well with its granite countertops and stainless steel appliances. Betty seemed to be a tasteful decorator as well.

As they talked, the two realized they had more in common than they had anticipated. Betty was a retired nurse, having worked at the city hospital for thirty years. "A lot has changed over time," Betty said. "The hospital has grown with the community, but it has always felt like a second home for our family. Paul's father was a surgeon there for many years. He passed away ten years ago. He was greatly admired by the people in the town, and Paul has followed in his footsteps."

"What happened to Paul's mother?" Melissa asked.

"Her name was Sarah," Betty replied. "She was my older sister. She went home to be with the Lord when Paul was in medical school. I came here to live with Paul and Lily after she passed away. Paul treats me like a mom and Lily like a grandmother. They are so sweet. I love them both dearly. We have had our share of tragedy in the Remington family, as you can see. Losing Evelyn suddenly three years ago was really hard on our family."

"Paul's wife?" Melissa asked.

"Yes," replied Betty. "You would have liked her, Melissa. She was full of life. She taught Sunday school at our church, and she also volunteered at the local women's shelter. She and Paul were inseparable," Betty sighed. There was a pause.

"May I ask what happened to her?" Melissa inquired.

Betty hesitated for a moment. "Paul would prefer I not tell you. He wouldn't want you to feel guilty."

"Feel guilty—but why?" Melissa asked.

"Paul's wife was killed by a stray bullet at a convenience store shooting. It has eaten away at him that he wasn't there for her. No doubt that was why he reacted so quickly when he saw you in danger. He didn't want anyone else to experience the pain of losing a loved one in that way. Paul is the kind of person who would risk his life to save someone in danger. Helping you has allowed him to get rid of guilt he has been carrying around since he lost Evelyn."

Melissa was quiet for some time as they worked together

in the kitchen. Seeing that her eyes had begun to water, Betty asked, "What is it, dear?"

"Paul has literally given me a second chance at life and I'm so grateful," Melissa answered.

Betty smiled. "Paul has that effect on people. He has saved many lives in the operating room."

"Has he come close to remarrying?" Melissa asked.

"Not in the least, dear," Betty answered. "I do my best but I can't replace Evelyn. I know Lily misses her Mom. Friends and family have been praying that the right person will come into their lives."

* * * * * * *

As the days turned into weeks, spring arrived in style. Melissa and Lily were having a great time preparing the flower beds for this year's annuals and perennials, while Paul watched from the balcony, a smile on his face. He knew Melissa was in for a treat—Lily was very passionate about gardening.

Melissa soon discovered that Lily was a walking encyclopedia of gardening. She took Melissa for an expert tour of the local nursery, naming everything from amaryllis to zinnia. Melissa laughed with pleasure as she followed her young friend around the greenhouse. At the end of the day, they came home with a dozen varieties of blooms.

The two friends went right to work planting their prized purchases. There were petunias, pansies, daisies, peonies, rhododendrons, and of course, lilies. Melissa noticed her little friend saved the lilies for last. "They are my favorite," she explained. "Daddy loves them too. I guess that's why he named me Lily."

"I think Lily is a beautiful name," said Melissa. "If I was

named after a flower, I wouldn't mind being named after a lily. Do you have a favorite?"

"Oh yes!" said Lily excitedly. "The coral lilies are my favorite. They were mom's favorite too," she said, showing her what they looked like. "Dad's favorite are the speckled raspberry," she stated, as she gave one to Melissa to place in the soil. "Which one do you like, Melissa?" Lily asked with keen interest.

Melissa looked over the large selection of colors. There were pink, plum, cream, white, bronze, purple, and rose lilies to choose from. "I think I like the rose-colored lilies the best," she said after a while.

"I knew it!" exclaimed Lily triumphantly. "I guessed right." Lily took a rose bloom and planted it in the soil next to a coral and raspberry. "The rose ones are my second favorite," she confided, with an inconspicuous tear in the corner of her eye.

* * * * * * *

On Sunday morning, Paul and Melissa, Lily, and Aunt Betty arrived at church and were welcomed by a friendly greeter. Lily and Betty led the way, clearing a path through the sea of humanity in the foyer. Paul followed, a cane on one side and Melissa on the other. So many people wanted to say hello to Paul that it took them awhile to make it to their seats.

"I feel like I'm with a celebrity." Melissa giggled. Though he was a little embarrassed by all the attention, Paul couldn't help laughing softly as well. Betty observed their joyful moment together as they walked down the aisle toward their seats.

Do either one of them know what they have? she wondered.

The sermon was barely underway when Melissa heard a familiar voice in her head. *Hello, daughter. It's good to see you back in My house. I haven't heard from you much lately. How are you doing?* the Lord whispered to her.

Melissa had grown up in church—the pastor's daughter. When her father had suddenly and unexpectedly died eight months earlier, she had been devastated. She had allowed the blow to take a toll on her spiritual life. Now, her heavenly Father was gently drawing her back to Him. A tear of thankfulness ran down her cheek.

"I am doing well, Lord. It is good to hear Your voice. Thank You for sending Paul to save my life," she whispered back. Just then she looked to her left, where Paul, Lily, and Betty were seated. "These are wonderful people," she continued. It's been a joy to get to know them."

Her gaze went back to Paul, who was looking straight ahead.

Paul is an honorable man, the Lord continued. Melissa agreed. *He needs a good wife.*

"I'm sure he will find a good woman one day, Lord," she responded.

I'm talking about you, Melissa. Paul needs you, the Lord said.

Melissa could hardly believe what she was hearing. God was playing matchmaker with her in church! Even so, Paul had something to say about all this. Did he see her as more than just a new acquaintance? She hoped so, but he'd done nothing to let her know.

"Lord, I don't think he cares for me that way. He was just being nice by helping me get back on my feet." She looked over at Lily affectionately. "Besides," she added, "my time with this family is almost up. I will be moving on soon."

Just then, Melissa caught herself. *This can't be real,* she thought. *Where in the Bible did God play matchmaker?*

How about Isaac and Rebekah, Ruth and Boaz, David and

Abigail, Joseph and Mary? came the reply. *Did I mention Adam and Eve? Would you like Me to keep going?*

"I get the message, Lord," Melissa finally conceded. *Time is running out, though,* she thought to herself.

Remember, my daughter, I know the end from the beginning, came the confident reply.

* * * * * * *

Paul, Lily, Betty, and Melissa were sitting around the den at the estate. Three months had passed without a single job opening for Melissa. She had no choice but to move back to Virginia. This was the beginning of saying good-bye.

"I would like to thank you for welcoming me into your home," she said to the small group who had once been acquaintances and were now as dear as family. "I've had the time of my life. I'll be taking back many fond memories to Virginia." It was a solemn moment.

Lily looked sad, but it was Betty who broke the unpleasant silence. "We understand, dear. We certainly have enjoyed having you here with us. Remember that you will always have friends here in Shiloh. Lily and I are going to the ice cream parlor for a treat. Would the two of you like to join us?"

"Thank you, Betty, but I'll pass," replied Paul.

"I still have some packing to do," added Melissa, as she got up to go to the bungalow.

As soon as Betty and Lily were out the front door, Melissa headed for the bungalow. She had heard Lily crying softly and it broke her heart. As she passed through the French door in the den, her conversation with the Lord in church seemed like a vague memory. She glanced back over her shoulder and saw Paul sitting in his chair deep in thought.

Not more than a few minutes after she arrived in the bungalow, the phone rang. "Hello?" she answered.

"Hello, Melissa. It's Paul. I was wondering if you would be interested in having dinner with me at Seashore, the Mediterranean restaurant in town?" he asked.

"What about Betty and Lily?" Melissa asked.

"They will be gone for quite a while, and there is plenty of food in the house," Paul countered. "I'm sure they won't mind."

Melissa took a deep breath and then agreed to Paul's invitation. Normally, she would have been excited about going out, but the prospect of saying good-bye had already been hard enough.

"I'll be ready in a few minutes," she said softly.

* * * * * * *

Paul and Melissa were greeted at the Seashore by Antonio, the restaurant owner. Paul had called in advance with a reservation. Antonio welcomed them both with a broad smile and open arms before escorting them to a quiet booth in a corner. The music and ambience were very relaxing.

Melissa recognized the rose-colored lilies in a vase as she sat down. She smiled with pleasure. "How did you know?" she asked Paul. "Oh, let me guess. A little bird told you!"

Paul smiled. "Lily mentioned the rose-colored ones are your favorite," he admitted. "I believe you will like the food here. Everything on the menu is exceptional."

* * * * * * *

A short while later, Betty and Lily arrived back at the house.

Betty was sipping a chocolate shake while Lily was working on a double scoop of chocolate chip and strawberry swirl. "Where is everyone?" Lily asked, as they entered the empty house. "Dad's car isn't in the driveway."

"This might tell us," Betty said as she picked up a note from the kitchen counter.

Dear Betty and Lily,
Melissa and I have gone to Seashore for dinner. See you soon.
Love,
Dad

"Oh my gosh, it's really happening!" exclaimed Betty. Lily looked confused.

"What is it, Betty?" Lily asked excitedly, trying to figure out what was happening. She took the note from Betty's hand and read it a couple of times.

"Dad hasn't gone to the Seashore for dinner since he took Mom before she died," Lily said. "This could only mean one thing." Hugging the piece of paper, Lily began to celebrate excitedly. "We have to go see them, Aunt Betty!" she insisted.

"We had best leave them alone," Aunt Betty answered. But Lily was having none of it.

"Please, Aunt Betty! I have to go see them! Please! Please!"

Finally Aunt Betty agreed. "Very well, then. Let's go!" she said as they headed out the door.

* * * * * * *

"You were right, Paul. The food was excellent," Melissa stated, as she finished her meal.

"I'm glad you liked it, Melissa," Paul answered. "I haven't

148

been here for a very long time," he added, looking at the rose lilies in the vase. There was a pause as though they were each instinctively preparing to receive the unknown. Then Paul ended the intimate silence.

"This is for you," he said. He pulled a velvet jewelry box out of his pocket, set it on the table in front of her, and slowly opened the lid. Inside was a beautiful diamond ring threaded by a coral lily and a raspberry lily. Paul could no longer contain the sea of emotions within. "Melissa, you needed me for a brief moment in your life. I need you for the rest of mine. *Please* say yes," he pleaded softly, passionately.

Melissa looked at the beautiful ring, and the two lilies that went with it. And then suddenly, Lily and Aunt Betty were there, smiling brightly. Seeing the ring and the two lilies, Lily held her breath as she and Paul waited for Melissa's answer.

Tears streamed down Melissa's face as she looked from Paul to Lily and nodded vigorously. Lily was no longer able to contain her excitement. She ran to Melissa with open arms. Melissa got on her knees and embraced Lily with all her heart.

"Yes! Yes! Yes!" she cried over and over again.

* * * * * * *

God sets the solitary in families.
Psalm 68:6

The Lion's Roar

There was a small team on a scientific expedition in the African forest. The three-member group consisted of a botanist, or plant specialist, and her two guides. The two guides were considered to be the best in the business and equal in ability.

The team spent the day studying plants and taking samples to bring back to the camp. The group got off course by the end of the day and was lost. There was a disagreement between the two guides regarding the way back to the safety of the camp. Remember, the two guides are equally qualified, but they disagree on which way the team should go. One guide tells the botanist the team should go left. The other guide insists they should turn right.

It is now dusk and getting dark. They hear a lion roaring in the distance through the thick brush.[1] The botanist discovers that one of her guides is a devout tither.[2] The other guide attends church but has never really bought into all that "tithing stuff." It is getting darker and the two guides are still in disagreement on the way back home. The guides separate from each other and start walking in opposite directions. The botanist hears the lion roaring again. Which guide should she follow?

[1] 1 Peter 5:8
[2] Malachi 3:10–11

The Mother's Prayer

The woman was alone in her house, on her knees praying.

"Dear Lord, thank You for watching over Hannah. I know, Lord, that she is in Your hands. Like the prodigal son, I know You are bringing my little girl home."

Wrong relationships had caused the teenager to rebel against her Christian upbringing. Last week she left home without warning. Warm tears ran down her mother's face as she poured out her soul to the Lord in the middle of the night.

"Heavenly Father," she continued, "I trust You with my little girl. I thank You for touching her heart. Thank You for reminding her how much I love her and how much You love her. Lord, I know she will come back and serve You all the days of her life."

She had been praying for more than an hour when there was a knock on the front door. The mother got up from her knees and went to see who was there. To her delight, she found her daughter standing under the porch light. Hannah was dirty and in need of a meal. Mother and daughter hugged with tears streaming down their faces.

"I'm so sorry, Mom. Please forgive me," Hannah said, holding on tight to her mother.

"I love you, honey," was all her mother could say. "I love you so much."

Hannah's mother brought her inside and the two of them

went straight to her mother's bedside. "Let's pray, honey," she told her daughter, as they both knelt beside the bed. Hannah demonstrated no surprise or resistance. She had grown up praying before bedtime.

"Dear Lord, thank You for opening my eyes and bringing me home. I only want Your will for my life now, Lord. From this day forward, I will live for You."

Hannah and her mother both stood up. "Mom, I have something to tell you," she started.

"What is it, honey?" her mother replied.

"Mom, I'm pregnant."

Hannah started going back to church with her mother. She never missed a service. She volunteered wherever help was needed. She was a different person now. She was also very beautiful. Several young men asked her to date, before it was obvious she was pregnant. She turned them all down. One fellow offered to marry her and raise the child as his own, but she declined. She was going to raise the child herself. Hannah spent many hours reading the Bible and singing songs to her unborn child. Like her mother, she had become a woman of prayer. One the day she learned her unborn child would be a son, she began praying this petition daily, "Lord, let him be a great soul winner."[1]

On the day her son was born, Hannah went into labor early in the morning. It was long and hard, as is the case with many first-time mothers. She pushed for two hours, making slow but steady progress. Finally, at eleven o'clock that night the baby came. It was only Hannah, her mother, the obstetrician, and two nurses in the birthing room. The baby came out crying, his arms moving everywhere. The doctor clamped and cut the umbilical cord. He placed the newborn on his mother's chest while the nurses wiped him dry.

"Thank You, Lord. Thank You," Hannah kept saying over and over. This child was going to grow up in a loving home.

But suddenly the atmosphere in the room changed. The obstetrician instructed a nurse to take the baby from Hannah for a while. Hannah's mother could tell by the concerned look on the doctor's face that something was wrong.

The doctor could not get the bleeding to stop after the placenta was delivered. Hannah's long, arduous labor had caused uterine atony or fatigue. The uterus would not contract, or clamp down, to stop the bleeding. A full-scale obstetric emergency was underway.

Hannah had lost IV access during pushing. The nurses tried frantically to start another IV but were having difficulty. One nurse massaged the uterus, while the other kept working to find a good vein. Hannah was given an injection of medication in her hip in an effort to stop the bleeding. Medical staff rushed in and out of the room. The doctor ordered two units of blood from the blood bank. But nothing was working. Hannah continued to bleed.

Soon the new mother was pale and losing consciousness. With a feeble breath she told her mother, "His name is Jeremiah." Hannah's mother began to cry along with the newborn baby under the warmer. Those were the last words she heard her daughter speak. "His name is Jeremiah.".

* * * * * * *

"Jeremiah…Jeremiah…Reverend Jeremiah." The man came out of his daydream. He was holding an old Bible in his hands. He had relived the scene of his birth thousands of times before. This was merely the latest episode. His grandmother had raised him after Hannah went home to be with the Lord.[2] As soon as he was old enough to understand, she had told him about his mother. Now in his thirties, the preacher looked down at the tattered Bible and read the inscription on the cover page. He knew it by heart. Every detail of every letter and word was etched in his mind.

> *To my beloved Jeremiah, mighty man of God. The Lord is with you always. I love you.*
> *Hannah*

"It is time, sir," his assistant informed him. Jeremiah stood up and walked to the back of the stage. A crowd of 300,000 souls were seated on the other side of the curtain. They had come to hear him speak about Jesus and the kingdom of God. Many had traveled for days, and multitudes were badly in need of God's healing touch.

Jeremiah realized he had been born for this moment. He had been called and ordained by God. He had been bathed in prayer from the womb. He was an anointed soul winner for the Lord Jesus Christ.[3] Jeremiah stood behind a small opening in the curtain. He looked out at the multitude and said a simple prayer to the Lord. As he spread the curtain open to enter the stage he whispered, "Thanks, Mom. I'll take it from here."

[1] Jeremiah 1:5
[2] Proverbs 22:6
[3] Isaiah 49:1–2

The Obituaries

Daphne Montgomery reclined in her bed, her gown drenched in sweat. Her two-week battle with the flu had sapped her strength. She felt she might be turning the corner, though—the fever and chills were gone at least. Her body still ached miserably, but her appetite was returning. She could hear Emily, the maid, bringing her breakfast and the London paper. The prospect of a tall glass of orange juice, some scrambled eggs, and the news sounded really good.

Emily was glad to see her mistress improving. She and her family had been serving the Montgomerys for three generations. Daphne lived alone in her luxurious estate on the city outskirts, close enough to keep her finger on London's business pulse. Her only daughter was married to an American sea merchant and lived in Boston. Emily was the closest thing to family Ms. Montgomery had in this part of the world.

"It's so good to see you eating again, Ms. Montgomery," Emily said, placing the breakfast tray on the end table.

"Me too," replied Daphne with a scratchy voice. "I really thought I was a goner this time. I guess I'm a tougher old bird than I thought." She softly laughed and coughed at that one.

Emily smiled too. "You're a very strong woman, ma'am. Dr. Evans was concerned about you, but I knew you would pull through."

Daphne eyed her maid fondly. "Thank you, dear. It's nice to

know someone was cheering for me."

Emily returned the compliment with a gentle bow of the head, and left the room, leaving Daphne with the paper on her lap and breakfast on the bedside table.

The meal invigorated the multi-millionaire businesswoman. She owned a steel mill, shipyard, real estate, and much more. Only her lawyer and accountant knew how much she was really worth. Her husband had died twenty years ago. She'd thought she'd marry again but she never had.

That might have had something to do with her nickname. In business circles, she was known as the Black Widow. The nickname bothered her at first, but she had grown accustomed to it. Everyone knew she was a shrewd business owner. Nobody pulled the wool over her eyes, and those who tried paid dearly. When it came to creating wealth, the Black Widow was considered brilliant, fearless, and even ruthless by those who knew her.

The Black Widow is back in action, she thought to herself, as she turned her full attention to the newspaper.

Daphne scanned the headlines with casual interest. She knew the real scoop behind many of the stories, but enjoyed the paper's rendition. She smiled as she worked her way to the business section—the only part that really interested her. Taking a look at the stock market page, she made some mental notes and decided to contact her broker soon.

She usually put the paper down after she finished the business pages, but today she moved on to the obituaries. *I wonder if any of my competitors cashed in their chips while I was down,* she thought. *Actually it could have been me this time. Heaven knows I felt like I was dying.*

Suddenly she saw something that took her breath away. Something she could never have anticipated. She rubbed her eyes and then looked again, but the face and the photo were still there.

Daphne Montgomery

Born April 26, 1930—Died February 11, 1999

Ms. Montgomery, the widow of wealthy corporate businessman Charles Montgomery, passed away at her London estate over the weekend, a victim of this year's flu epidemic. The eccentric and solitary millionaire was also known as the "Black Widow" for her opportunistic takeovers and penchant for closing down small family businesses. Mrs. Montgomery was not known to give to charities, and working conditions at her steel mill and shipyard were considered dismal. She is survived by her daughter, Judith, who lives in Boston. Ms. Montgomery will probably be best remembered for her business slogan, "Making money is all that matters."

Daphne read her obituary several times, a task that became increasingly painful. She quickly noticed that not a single good word had been said about her. She put the paper down and looked straight ahead. *Is this how I am going to be remembered?* she thought. A silent tear rolled down her right cheek. *What have I become?* she whispered.

Just then there was a knock on her bedroom door. "Come in," said Ms. Montgomery, trying to regain her composure. It was Emily, and she had someone with her.

"Begging your pardon, ma'am, but you have a visitor. It's

the Reverend Jones, ma'am."

The pastor of the Methodist church Mrs. Montgomery had long attended walked in with a smile and sat down at her bedside.

"Hello, Daphne! Glad to see you're still with us. I read your obituary this morning and was pleasantly surprised to find that you are not dead at all—but alive and improving! How are you doing?"

Daphne was a mixed bag of emotions. "I am well. No, I am not! Did you see what they wrote about me?" she exclaimed, as she threw the paper at the foot of the bed.

Reverend Jones, in his mid-forties, had known Daphne most of his life. They had been friends for a long time. Along with Emily, he was the closest thing to family she had as well. "Thomas, they had no right to say those things about me in the obituary! Who wants a legacy like that?"

"I was sad to read the things they wrote about you in the paper. I'm also sorry to hear that you're hurting as a result. I knew you would be. Deep down, Daphne, I know you have feelings. I also know you don't wish to be remembered the way you were portrayed in this obituary," he said, glancing at the newspaper.

"But what can I do to change at this point?" she asked. Reverend Jones looked at her with great compassion. "His name is Jesus. All you have to do is make room in your heart for Him." He took her hand and asked if she was ready to take the first step. For the first time in her life, Daphne realized she needed God more than anything else in this world.

"Yes," she replied softly. They prayed together, Reverend Jones leading the way. "Lord Jesus, I need You in my life. I need Your gentle touch and healing power. I open my heart and ask You to come in. Have Your way in my life. Fill me with Your

Spirit. Thank You. Amen."

Thomas looked at his old friend affectionately and stood up. "We'll be seeing you in church when you're feeling better," he assured her as he exited.

Daphne, left alone in her room, did not hear the Lord speak words to her heart. She did not need words at that moment. She felt His warmth and love come upon her instead. She closed her eyes, basking in the glory of His presence, tears streaming down her face. The Great Physician began cleansing her wounds and making her well. Daphne started sobbing deeply and uncontrollably. Emily could hear her mistress through the thick bedroom door, and knew not to disturb her. It would take some time to uncover all the layers of hurt.

Daphne stayed home to recover for thirty days. She had breakfast in bed the first week until she was strong enough to go for walks around her estate. She prayed in the mornings, read her Bible throughout the day in different parts of the mansion, and took walks in the garden. Her lawyer and accountant came over periodically to discuss business. Reverend Thomas and his wife, Joanna, visited Ms. Montgomery every other day for Bible study. They shared some wonderful moments together. They prayed, read the Word, and laughed together. One month seemed like one week.

Daphne was a new woman after her bout with the flu. The accidental obituary had made a crucial difference and helped her resurrect her life. Daphne's heart of stone had been replaced with a heart of flesh.[1] She saw the world through different eyes.

She worked to improved the working conditions at the steel mill and the shipyard, and raised wages across the board. In addition, she made a substantial contribution to a women's college on the east side of London. In the evenings, she taught a class for small business owners free of charge. She poured her fifty years of business acumen into her students, and even introduced them to some of her wealthy business associates and competitors. They were all baffled and somewhat amused by the changes they were seeing in the former Black Widow.

Daphne also found time to rally support for a top-notch orphanage and opened her home at Christmas for the children to enjoy caroling, eating, games, and presents. Ms. Montgomery was more than a changed person, she was a happy person!

Ms. Daphne lived another eleven years—a long life[2]— before dying quietly in her sleep. The large Methodist church was packed for her memorial service. People from all over London attended the proceedings. Emily and Joanna sat together in the front while Reverend Thomas Jones did the tribute. He couldn't help but think about the message he would have delivered to a much smaller audience a decade before. God had used the flu and a newspaper snafu to give Daphne a second chance to change her life and the lives of others.

At the end of his message, Reverend Jones pulled two pieces of paper out of his coat pocket and set them on the pulpit. He shared the story of Ms. Montgomery's near fatal bout with the flu and premature obituary. Everyone laughed. He then proceeded to read the first obituary to the audience. Those who had known Daphne only in recent years could hardly believe he was talking about the same person. "Like Zacchaeus, she made room in her heart for Jesus and salvation came to her house," he said. [3]

Reverend Jones then raised the second piece of paper for the audience to see. "This is Ms. Daphne's second obituary written a few days ago. I would like to read it to you now."

Daphne Montgomery
Born April 26, 1930—Died August 11, 2010

Ms. Montgomery, the widow of wealthy corporate businessman Charles Montgomery, passed away in her sleep at her London estate over the weekend. She used much of her great wealth to touch the lives of people in our community and around the world. She was a mentor for the underdog, a big sister to women, a voice for the afflicted, a shelter for the homeless, and a warm meal for the hungry. Ms. Daphne, as those who loved her best always called her, will be well remembered for her kindness, generosity, and gentle spirit. She obtained a good testimony through her faith.[4]

"What will others say about you one day?" Reverend Jones concluded. "God's grace gives us an opportunity to rewrite our obituaries."

[1] Ezekiel 36:26
[2] Psalm 91:16
[3] Luke 19:8–10
[4] Hebrews 11:39–40

The Perfect Rose

The king's carriage made its way through the streets of Begohla on its monthly tour of the capital city. People lined the streets to get a glimpse of his majesty, King Dorin, waving as he passed by with his entourage of mounted horsemen. Lord Edgaar, the Chief Counselor, rode in the open carriage at the king's side. The driver turned to the right down a familiar street lined with shops, restaurants, and small businesses. People waved, applauded, and shouted with approval at their beloved monarch.

A slender man stood in front of a metal smith shop with a young girl by his side. His clothes and hands were dirty from hard work, but he bowed with reverence as the royal procession approached. The little girl threw a red rose onto the street in front of the king's carriage and bowed like her father. King Dorin noticed the little girl immediately and was touched by the child's beautiful gesture. He nodded his head ever so slightly in acknowledgement of the metal smith and then smiled down at the girl standing next to him. "Did you see that, Lord Edgaar?" he asked, indicating the little girl and her father.

"Why, yes, Your Majesty," Lord Edgaar replied.

King Dorin could not forget the sweet little girl and her red rose, blue eyes, and walnut-brown hair. She had melted his heart.

* * * * * * *

"The king will see you now," the servant told the man waiting outside Dorin's study at the palace. He opened the door to a massive, two-story library with a spiral staircase and indoor wrap-around balcony. Having been summoned to the palace, the metal smith had washed and put on his most presentable clothes. His hands, however, would always carry the obvious signs and scars from years of hard labor. *What could the king possibly want with me?* he asked himself.

King Dorin sat at a large, leather-top desk with gold trim signing documents. "Come in, Reese, come in." The king beckoned with a smile. The metal smith was made more at ease by King Dorin's friendly welcome, but he still could not imagine why he was here. He approached the king slowly and bowed his head before him. "Good afternoon, Your Majesty," he said.

The king got up from his chair and came around his desk to shake Reese's hand. He gave his visitor a warm smile. "It's good to see you, old friend! It has been a long while. Please, sit down, won't you?" he said, gesturing to a comfortable wing-back chair. The king sat in his large leather seat behind his desk.

"Thank you, Your Majesty," Reese replied, taking his chair. It was good to both see and speak with Dorin once again. They had grown up together as childhood friends, lads from the same neighborhood, hearing their lessons together, playing games, fishing, and exploring. Obviously their adult lives had gone in different directions. Dorin had become a soldier and eventually king. Reese had taken a more expected route, learning his father's profession, marrying, and raising a family.

"Please, Reese, let's dispense with the 'Your Majesty' business. Just call me Dorin. After all, we are practically family."

Reese smiled. He appreciated the gesture and Dorin's continued friendship over the years. He was, however, a man of strong tradition and honor, and Dorin was his king. He could not bring himself to address the king in such a familiar way.

"Thank you, King Dorin. I appreciate the gesture and think of you most fondly, but my honor will not allow me to address you as anything other than Your Majesty."

"Whatever you are comfortable with," Dorin replied with understanding. His old friend was humble and mild-mannered as always. "I wonder, though, how is your health, my friend?"

Reese lowered his head with sadness. "My heart is failing, Your Majesty. The doctors tell me I don't have many years left. My wife has been gone now for several years, but I have not cared to remarry."

"What of your daughter?" Dorin asked.

"My little Aurora and I live in a small room behind my shop. But when I'm gone she will have to live with one of my brothers or sisters quite some distance from here. They are good people, but I hate to think of her leaving all she has ever known. It's bad enough that she lost her mother at such an early age. I hope she will not lose me as well before she has had a chance to grow up and marry."

A single tear streamed down the man's face. There was a brief, tangible silence between them. Dorin remembered again the young girl with the red rose standing next to her father.

"I wish to give you my promise, Reese," King Dorin stated. "You will never have to worry about anything again. I have asked my servants to prepare a place for you here in the palace. You and Aurora can help me in the garden. Everything you could possibly need will be provided for you, including the finest education Aurora could receive. And I give you my word, Reese—should anything happen to you, I will care for Aurora as if she were my own."

A stream of tears covered Reese's face from relief and gratitude. "Thank you, Your Majesty!: "Reese exclaimed. "I don't know what to say in response to such kindness and generosity!"

"All you need do is accept, Reese. It's the least I can do for an old comrade and his precious little girl." As King Dorin rose from his chair, Reese did the same out of respect. The king came around his desk and gave his loyal friend and subject a big, compassionate hug.

* * * * * * *

King Dorin was enjoying his daily stroll in the royal gardens. The grounds were more beautiful than ever thanks to the oversight Aurora had given them over the years. She and a team of gardeners, working under her supervision, kept the property in pristine condition. In addition, the young woman exercised her love for learning. Not only was she proficient in four languages, she also studied mathematics, economics, music, literature—of which botany was, of course, her favorite. After time spent with her books and piano, she was always anxious to get out into the garden and practice her craft.

On this day, King Dorin found her near a large fountain pruning a rose bush. When she noticed his presence, she looked up and smiled. It was, in his opinion, the most beautiful smile he had ever seen, the same one he had fallen in love with so many years ago while riding through town in his carriage.

"There you are, my dear!" he said to her. "It's so good to see you. Come, take a break from your task and walk with me."

Aurora left her spade and apron behind and joined the king. Wrapping her hand around his arm like a loving daughter, the two of them set off. King Dorin had become a second father to her after Reese was gone. He loved her like his own child. "Tell me, dear. How is it you make the garden seemingly more beautiful every year?" he asked. "You have truly outdone yourself this time, my sweet Aurora. My visitors always ask the name of my impressive gardener."

Aurora smiled and blushed at the compliment. "Oh, you are just saying that, Your Majesty," she teased. "I really don't do that much. I just provide a little direction here and there. You have a symphony of talented groundskeepers, who do all the real work."

"Ah yes, my, child," Dorin replied. "You, however, are the maestro and my garden is your masterpiece. I hope word does not get around. I might be forced to raise your wages in order to keep you on here at the palace," he said playfully.

Aurora smiled, eyes watering slightly. "That won't be necessary, Your Majesty. A hug from you every morning is all the wages I need," she replied affectionately. She rested her head on his shoulder as they walked. Dorin felt his heart melting again. Aurora had a way of doing that to him on a regular basis. She meant everything to him.

"My dear Aurora. You are like the daughter I never had. You are the most beautiful rose in my garden." His eyes became moist, lips quivering ever so slightly. "Now run off before you make this sentimental, old man cry," he added playfully.

Aurora gave him an affectionate smile. "Very well," she said. She gave him a kiss on the cheek and disappeared in a maze of bushes and vines. Dorin watched her go, sighing deeply, hoping he could experience moments like this the rest of his life. Everything in the world seemed perfect and right after a walk in the garden with his precious Aurora.

* * * * * * *

The small table on the patio by the pond was prepared for supper. A cut glass vase with fresh flowers provided by Aurora decorated the table. King Dorin savored his meal as the sun began to disappear behind the horizon. This was an important meeting.

"I am not getting any younger, Jayden. You are the only heir to the throne. It is time to start thinking about starting your own family," the king instructed Jayden, his only son.

The young prince washed down the last piece of his roasted pork with some water. He looked up at his father, knowing he had his best interests in mind. But there had been little time to spare after tending to his other responsibilities as heir to the throne. In fact, he had just returned from a three-month trip to finalize peace negotiations with the kingdom of Quohl. These precious moments back home with his father were rare indeed.

But Jayden also understood the importance of having a good royal consort. His father was right. It *was* time to start searching for a companion to help him continue the royal line. The demands of education, military service, and royal duties had not allowed time for relationships with women. To put it simply, Jayden was inexperienced and naïve about those mysterious creatures. Nonetheless, he knew he had to choose one with whom he would spend the rest of his life. He wished his mother, Queen Arista, was alive to give him advice. He scratched his head apprehensively as he addressed his father.

"I know this is something I must do…soon, my father. I

have to confess, though, I am at a loss where to start. I don't even know what I'm looking for. It would help if you could give me some advice. Do you know someone who would make a successful wife for me?" he asked. King Dorin laughed softly and looked at his son with affection.

"Jayden, there are many fine young women in the empire who would make a good queen. It is your responsibility to find the woman that will make a *great* one." Dorin saw Aurora in the distance, bringing a second course of food. She was wearing a pale green dress that flowed in symphony with her long, wavy hair. He smiled at her from a distance as he continued his conversation with Jayden.

"Son, I can't help you here. This must be your decision and yours alone. A king must be able to see into the souls of his people and sympathize with their hopes and dreams, hurts and disappointments. How can you know what your people need when you do not even know what it is *you* need?" he asked.

Jayden opened his mouth to speak, but Dorin continued without letting him get a word in. He gazed at Aurora approaching, still out of earshot.

"Son, you will be ready to rule when you find the woman who is able to become a great queen." His voice softened and his eyes watered as Aurora approached. Jayden was somewhere else, deep in thought at his father's words. Dorin continued. "You will be ready to be king when you can identify the perfect rose," he concluded softly, looking into Aurora's beautiful blue eyes and radiant smile. He smiled back at her.

"Does anyone have room for venison?" she asked playfully in her soft, melodic voice. Jayden came out of his trance, startled by her sudden arrival.

"There you are, my dear! Please join us," the king insisted. "Jayden and I were just discussing an important matter. We are trying to find him a suitable consort."

Aurora set the meat and steaming vegetables on the table. She gazed at Jayden quizzically as she began to slice them generous portions of succulent meat, potatoes, and corn. "As a woman of unusual grace and wisdom, you may be able to advise Jayden as to what characteristics he might look for, my dear."

Jayden was delighted to see Aurora. "So good to see you," he stated warmly. "I hardly recognize you these days. Each time I return from my journeys, you seem to have grown so much."

Aurora smiled and blushed slightly.

Dorin was enjoying himself thoroughly. *Open your eyes, Jayden!* he thought to himself, and with that he excused himself.

"I will leave you with Jayden to help him solve this great dilemma," he told Aurora, chuckling. "I have business matters I need to attend to. Jayden, listen to what she tells you. I do, and it keeps me out of a lot of trouble." Aurora giggled at the king's compliment. He winked at her as he got up to leave. Jayden was a fine young man, but he seemed to have no common sense when it came to women.

"Lord, help him," King Dorin whispered as he walked back to the palace, thinking about his son.

Jayden motioned for Aurora to have a seat at the table. She was like a sister to him in many ways. She had grown up in the palace with him and enjoyed many of the same privileges he did. She had been raised as a princess in every way with the exception of her birth and early childhood. The two had enjoyed playing pranks on each other as brothers and sisters often do. But suddenly and for the first time, Jayden saw a different person sitting across from him. Aurora had grown into a beautiful woman. Why had he not noticed before?

Jayden suppressed a growing sense of attraction as he spoke to her. "Please stay awhile Aurora, and eat with me. Father is right. I desperately need some womanly advice on finding a suitable mate."

Aurora gazed at Jayden affectionately along with a tinge of sorrow. Besides King Dorin, Jayden had been in her life more than anyone else she knew. Aurora had had a girl's crush on Jayden since the day she met him in the royal stables feeding horses. She had never shared her feelings with anyone. It was obvious to everyone in the palace, however, that Aurora cared deeply for Jayden. Now he was asking *her* for advice to find a royal consort. This was proving to be difficult for her. The conversation was bittersweet in her heart. She sighed softly.

"Well, Jayden, since you have asked for my opinion, I will oblige you," she started, managing a slight smile. "I believe a queen should be loyal, industrious, resourceful, and intelligent. She must be compassionate towards the poor, creative, honorable, wise, kind, and a good mother. Lastly, and most importantly, she must be a God-fearing woman." There was a brief pause as Jayden took in everything Aurora said.

"Shouldn't physical beauty play a part?" he asked.

Aurora looked at him sympathetically. "True beauty comes from within, Jayden. When you marry a woman who is beautiful on the inside, she will always be beautiful to you on the outside," she concluded.

Jayden took Aurora's hand and gave it an affectionate, grateful squeeze. He was thankful for the advice. Perhaps finding the right woman would not prove to be so difficult after all. "You have given me a lot to think about, Aurora. I would like to ask you to do something for me. When I have found someone, can you tell me if you think she is the right one?" he asked as he got up to leave.

Aurora's soul was in agony. She mustered up the strength to reply. "I am sorry, Jayden, but that is something I cannot do. Only your heart can tell you if she is the right one," she said softly, trying to suppress a tear.

"Thank you again for the advice you have given me today, Aurora. I am grateful." Jayden stood up to leave, but first he bent down and kissed Aurora affectionately on the forehead. Then he turned and walked toward the palace.

Aurora looked at Jayden as he got farther and farther away. "You are welcome," she whispered. "I hope you will find who you are looking for," she said. "Someone who will be a proper queen and someone who will love you with all her heart."

* * * * * * * *

Jayden sat in the piano room on the third floor, overlooking the royal gardens. Glenko, his assistant, took notes as he and his fiance, Lady Corelia, made plans for their royal wedding. Jayden stole a look at his soon-to-be bride. No doubt about it, Corelia was a magnificent woman by any man's standards. She was stunningly beautiful, with long chestnut hair and hazel eyes. Her soft, delicate voice was like music to the soul. She was educated, regal, and always conducted herself with the utmost propriety. Jayden had chosen her from among the fairest women in the kingdom. Noticing that he was looking her way, Corelia countered with an affectionate smile.

This is perfect, Jayden whispered to himself. And it was—all except for a small, persistent tug deep inside him. It had been there from the beginning and he couldn't seem to put it to rest. He got up from the velvet couch and walked to the window, restless but unable to understand why. He was looking down on the royal gardens where he and his betrothed would share afternoon tea, when he saw her. It was only a glimpse, but his heart suddenly began to beat faster and the palms of his hands began to sweat. *What's going on with me?* he wondered.

Then she came into view once again—sweet, kind, and thoughtful Aurora was preparing tea for Jayden and Corelia. It was not her responsibility but she had always insisted on serving him tea whenever he was home. Now she was quietly doing her best for the two of them, as well as placing a vase of beautifully arranged flowers on the table for their enjoyment.

As Jayden continued to watch, he noticed something unexpected. Aurora, her task finished, walked slowly to the edge of the large fountain in the center of the garden. She sat down slowly, no trace of a smile on her lips. Not only that but she seemed to be weeping. Jayden watched as she dabbed tears from her eyes. *Who has done harm to sweet Aurora?* he wondered. *Who could be cruel to such a beautiful creature?*

Without warning, Jayden found himself welling up with anger. And then his anger was replaced by sorrow as he remembered his father's words. *A king must be able to see into the souls of his people and sympathize with their hopes and dreams, hurts, and disappointments. How can you know what your people need when you do not even know what it is that you need? Son, you will be ready to rule when you find the woman who will make a great queen. You will be ready to be king when you can identify the perfect rose.*

In a moment of singular insight, Jayden understood the meaning of his father's words. He had caught a glimpse into Aurora's soul. He had been too blind to see the signs for all these years, though they were right in front of him. This woman cared for him, loved him, and though he had only just realized it—he cared for her as well. Suddenly the quiet tug inside was replaced by a burning ember. Aurora was his perfect rose.

Jayden snapped back to reality only to see Corelia standing by his side. She, too, was staring down at Aurora. For some time, neither of them spoke. Then Jayden looked into Corelia's sad eyes. "I am so sorry," he said. "I have moved too quickly and now I am going to disappoint you. I cannot go through with this wedding. As wonderful as you are, I realize now that my heart belongs to someone else."

How Corelia knew, he wasn't sure—but she did. She could see the truth in his eyes perhaps. But she didn't become angry to go into crying. Instead, she looked up at him with a faint smile and said, "Go to her. You must. Even I can see that it's the right thing to do."

Jayden dashed out of the piano room, down the spiral stairwell toward the gardens. As Glenko and Corelia watched from above, the young prince hurried to Aurora's side. He was so overcome with emotion as he took her in his arms that he could not speak a word, but he didn't have to. Aurora knew and her heart simply took flight.

* * * * * * * *

At long last, Jayden took Aurora by the hand and together they sat down on the bench next to the fountain.

"I believe I am the cause of your sorrow, Aurora, is that not so?" Unable to speak, she squeezed his hand. "Please allow me to be the cause of your joy," he said, like a soft ocean breeze.

"But how can it be? What about Lady Corelia?" she asked quietly.

"She gave me leave to come," he answered. "She could see that you are the only one who has claim to my heart. You are my perfect rose."

Aurora surrendered to the only man she ever loved. Two souls embraced as one in a bond of love and passion beyond any dream imaginable. The perfect rose and the one to whom she was destined to belong.

The Prettiest Girl

Andrew Davis looked out the living room window to the next farm over. He held his gaze for quite some time, deep in thought. So deep in fact that he didn't notice when his mother walked into the room.

"What is it you're looking at so intently?" Daisy asked her sixteen-year-old son in her soft Southern voice. Daisy and Andrew had always had a close relationship, but this was something she couldn't interpret.

Andrew turned from the window and looked straight into his mother's eyes. "Well, I suppose I've kept it to myself long enough," he said. "I think I'm in love—with Tricia Holcombe. I think I have been for quite some time. I can't hardly think about anything else."

He felt relieved to get this secret out in the open, but he was taken back by his mother's response. First she smiled. Then she gave him a big hug! Andrew took a deep breath and then they both turned to the window and stared out at the Holcombe farm together.

The Davises and Holcombes had lived side by side peacefully for more than sixty years. Tricia's mother, LeAnn, was one of Daisy's closest friends and prayer partners. They visited frequently while the kids were in school. What those kids didn't know is that their moms often talked about their kids getting married one day. That would make them even closer than friends. They would become family. Daisy was bubbling over with delight at Andrew's confession.

"Tricia is a beautiful, sweet girl, Andy. We have known her family for a long time. They are wonderful people." There was a pause before Daisy continued. "Maybe you should tell Tricia how you feel about her."

"I don't know if I can do that, Mom," he replied somewhat anxiously. "First of all, she's beautiful, and second, she's a year older than me. What if she laughs? What if she doesn't love me back? Besides, I'm just a homeschool geek! What could she possibly see in me?"

Daisy sighed deeply. "Son, you are a fine young man—intelligent, handsome, polite, and hard-working. You would make any girl with half a mind happy. One year difference in age is nothing," she added. "Your dad is younger than me—three years, not just one. You won't know until you find the courage to ask her out on a date," Daisy concluded.

His mother always made Andrew feel he could accomplish anything, even asking Tricia Holcombe out on a date. He could feel his confidence rising a little.

Daisy could sense the same thing. She had an idea. She went to the kitchen and came back with one of the two apple pies she had baked the night before and handed it to Andrew.

"Here you go, Andrew. Take this next door to LeAnn. Tricia is already home from school. This doesn't have to be complicated. Just ask her if she'd like to go with you to Brandi's Snow Cone Palace for a burger and ice cream. I'm certain she will say yes."

"Gee, I don't know, Mom—" Andrew started. But Daisy wasn't going to take no for an answer. She handed Andrew the pie and nudged him out the screen door.

"Tell LeAnn I said hello," she shouted as Andrew walked

down the dirt road to the Holcombes' place. She hurriedly closed the door behind her, picked up the phone, and started dialing. After a couple of rings a woman's voice said, "Holcombe residence."

"LeAnn, this is Daisy. Don't say anything, just listen! Andy is coming over with an apple pie I baked for you all. He wants to ask Tricia out on a date, but he's very shy. You have to help him!"

Now it was LeAnn's turn to be excited. This is what the two friends had been praying for. She glanced out the window in time to see Andrew walking up the driveway. As soon as he got to the top of the steps, she swung the door open.

"Well, hello, Andy. What are you up to, sweetie?"

Andrew smiled. Mrs. Holcombe always made him feel right at home.

"My mom baked this for you last night, Mrs. H. She asked me to bring it over to you," he added, looking around for any signs of Tricia. LeAnn smiled ever so slightly as she took the pie and placed it on the counter.

"Why thank you, dear. Please tell your mom how grateful I am. It was nice of you to bring it over," she said, taking him by the arm, turning him around, and walking him out to the porch swing. Several large trees in the front yard provided shade from the sun. "You just have a seat. I'll be right back," she said.

Mrs. H. quickly returned with two tall glasses of iced tea, which Andrew gladly accepted. His throat was suddenly as dry as sawdust. Daisy watched with binoculars as LeAnn took a seat in a recliner to Andrew's left.

LeAnn had to say something to break the ice and get the conversation going in the right direction. "Mr. Holcombe and Daryl went into town to get a few things from the hardware store. But Tricia is upstairs in her room doing homework. I'll let her know you're here," she said as she started to get up.

"Please don't do that! At least not yet," Andrew pleaded, a little more excitedly than he intended. His heart was racing and his breathing had picked up. LeAnn feigned surprise.

"Why not, Andy? Whatever is the matter, dear?" she inquired encouragingly. Andrew could feel himself getting calmer thanks to her.

"I've already told my mom. I guess I can tell you too, Mrs. Holcombe. I think Tricia is the prettiest girl I've ever seen. I would like to ask Tricia to go with me to the Snow Cone Palace. Do you think she would like to do that?" he asked. Andrew looked at Mrs. Holcombe intently, hanging on every facial expression.

When Mrs. H. gave Andrew a smile, he felt a new surge of confidence.

"Tell you what. I'm going to go inside and start dinner. I'll ask Tricia to come down and visit with you. And don't worry, Andy. You're one of the finest young men I know. I'm sure Tricia would be delighted to go on a date with you." She reached over and squeezed his hand before getting up. "Just be yourself, dear!"

Andrew smiled and nodded. He watched as Mrs. H. opened the screen door and went back into the house, and he could hear her calling Tricia from the bottom of the stairs. He took a few deep breaths to try to settle his nerves. Then he sat and waited for the most beautiful girl in the world to come out the front door. About half a minute later, she did.

Tricia would have made any young man's heart beat faster. She had cascading blond hair and a beautiful smile. Her light olive skin and pale blue eyes took Andrew's breath away. She was wearing long blue jeans, soft leather shoes, and a light pink cotton blouse.

"Hi Andy," she said warmly. He loved the sound of her voice.

This situation was new, but being around Tricia wasn't. Their families often sat together in church and went out for lunch together after the service. Andy visited the Holcombe's on a regular basis, but somehow, this seemed different.

"Mom said you wanted to talk to me," Tricia said.

"Uh yes, that's right," he began, surprised by the sound of his own voice. "I was wondering if—"

Suddenly, a new black mustang pulled up to the driveway, honking its horn. It was Jesse Clark, the high school quarterback and most popular guy in school. His parents were wealthy and lived in a mansion in Dover. He was also in the same youth group as Tricia and Andrew.

"Hey, Tricia! How would you like to go for a spin in my new wheels?" he shouted at her from the driver's seat. And just like that, she was up and moving.

"Sure, Jesse!" she called back. Then she called to her mother through the screen door, "Mom, I'll be back in a few minutes!"

Tricia started down the porch stairs and then remembered Andy sitting there on the swing. "Oh Andy, I'm so sorry. What did you want to ask me?" she said.

"It was nothing, Tricia. It can wait. Have a nice time," he blurted out. No way could he compete with a black mustang and a football quarterback. He conjured up a smile.

Tricia smiled back. "Sounds good. We'll see you soon!" she said, already halfway to the car. She waved as she got into the passenger seat and Andy watched them take off in a cloud of dust.

* * * * * * *

The red double-cabin truck pulled up the Davis' driveway and parked in front of the house. The driver got out of the vehicle and made his way to the front door. An old golden retriever greeted him joyfully as usual. He patted Chester on the head before opening the door. As he walked inside, he shouted playfully, "Is anybody home!"

Daisy called out from the kitchen. "Andy! Is that you?" She knew it had to be and almost tripped as she raced to the foyer to give her son an enormous hug. Her Andrew was home for good.

"I can hardly believe it! I've been on pins and needles waiting for you to get here. And this time, you're home to stay!" She reached up and gave him a kiss on the cheek. "Come sit down, my Andy. I can't tell you how happy I am to finally have you back. Eight years is a long time to wait. But here you are finally with college and vet school in the bag and only good things ahead!" She took his arm and led him into the living room where they sat down on the sofa. Daisy continued the conversation.

"I have a surprise for you. Mrs. Keller has helped me redecorate your room, and there's more. We're throwing a coming home party for you on Saturday. I've planned all your favorite meals as well. Your dad will be up from the barn real soon. He can hardly wait for you to join his practice. Father and son working side-by-side. How perfect is that?!"

Andrew was soaking it all in. *It's true what they say—there's no place like home,* he thought.

"Everyone at church has been asking me about you," Daisy continued.

Andy looked out the living room window to his right--toward the Holcombes' place. *Has Tricia asked about me?* he thought to himself. Daisy followed the direction of his gaze. "How is Tricia doing?" he asked.

His mother sighed softly. "I believe she's better now. She's finally free of that husband of hers. I knew when she married that Clark boy right after high school that things were probably not going to go well for her. But she thought she was in love. Of course, he had no intention of getting an education or making anything of himself. A spoiled rich kid is what he was. Of course, we take marriage seriously around here. We all prayed that somehow he would come around and they would be able to make a go of it. But it didn't happen. Instead, he continued to drink, and poor Tricia got the worst of it. After a couple of years, he left her—took off and moved to Nashville. Someone told me he'd been injured in a bar fight, but we don't hear much about him nowadays. Tricia finally divorced him."

Andrew's heart ached at the thought of Tricia's unhappiness. He remembered that day on her front porch, all ready to ask her out, and then watching as she drove off in Jesse Clark's mustang.

"What about Tricia now? What is she doing these days?" he asked, trying to sound casual about it.

Daisy perked up. "Well—she's come a long way. After her marriage failed, she could have just checked out of life—immersed in her disappointment. But instead she got a degree from Hampton College and now she's helping her parents run their feed store. She's involved with the youth at church. She's been able to use her experiences to help a lot of young girls make better choices than she did. She's quite a remarkable young lady," she said, eyeing Andrew closely.

"You're right, Mom. She always was remarkable," he

agreed. There was brief silence before he continued. "Is she seeing anyone these days?" Andy knew Tricia had married Jesse Clark. He'd tried to get her out of his heart by focusing on the demands of his schooling. He'd even tried to find someone else, another relationship—but finally he'd realized that all roads led back to Tricia. He would have to respect her decision to marry someone else, but he knew he would always love her.

Daisy Davis knew her son. Tricia Holcombe was still in his system.

"No, dear. Tricia is not seeing anyone. Her mother says she's decided to put romance on the back burner for now, but she's still a beauty. Someone is going to snatch her up one of these days. No doubt about that!"

There was a lengthy pause as Daisy's words settled in. "You know, Andy, she asks about you all the time," his mother added.

"She does?" he asked with surprise.

"Yes, dear. She hasn't forgotten you."

Andrew got up to his feet suddenly and marched toward the front door. "I'll be back in soon, Mom," he said without offering further explanation.

Daisy looked concerned. Had she upset him? "Where are you going, dear?" she asked.

Andrew looked back at her and smiled. "As the new veterinarian in town, I need to check out the local feed store. I'll be back soon," he said with a wink.

* * * * * *

"Tricia, can you pass me a pen, please?" her mother asked, smiling at Mrs. Cunningham, who was about to sign a check for her animal supplies.

The woman took the pen and signed with a flourish. "Here

you go," she said.

Ms. Holcombe answered with a smile. "Have a nice day, Barbara," she said, as her friend and customer made her way to the front door.

Just then, a tall, good-looking man opened the glass door for her and walked in the store unnoticed. "Can one of you ladies tell me where I can get some premium dry dog food?" he asked, smiling.

"Andy!" they both shouted in unison. Mrs. Holcombe and Tricia left the counter area to greet him with hugs. It was definitely good to be back home.

"Daisy told me you were coming back soon, dear." Andrew never tired of hearing Mrs. Holcombe call him *dear*. Tricia looked on with a smile on her face.

"Yes, ma'am. I'm here to stay." He looked into Tricia's captivating blue eyes. He knew what he wanted in life. The last ten years had taught him that. He pulled something out of a plastic bag he was carrying.

"I got this for you, Mrs. Holcombe. It's an apple pie from the Heartland Bakery. I hope you don't mind if it's not homemade," he added.

"I don't mind one bit." LeAnn laughed.

Andrew turned his attention to Tricia. Here they were— older and wiser.

"You know, Mrs. Holcombe, your Tricia is still the prettiest girl I've ever seen," Andy said, never taking his eyes off of his long-time love. "And I've waited far too long to ask an important question. Miss Tricia Holcombe, would you like to go with me to Brandi's for some ice cream?" he asked.

"Do I get all the butter pecan I want?" Tricia said playfully.

"You can have all the butter pecan you want the rest of your life if you say yes," he replied.

The Real Superwoman

The real Superwoman walked into my office sixteen weeks pregnant. She wasn't wearing a big letter *S* across her chest or anything like that. I only found out who she was during the course of her new OB visit. I am not talking about the make-believe, pretend Superwoman in comic books and cartoons. I am talking about the *real* Superwoman. I am referring to a living, breathing, remarkable, extraordinary, bigger-than-life woman of steel. What does the *real* Superwoman look like? I am so glad you asked.

The real Superwoman was about five feet four, average build, dirty blond hair, and light brown eyes. She was disguised as a military wife, architect, and mother of three with one on the way. Remarkably, she didn't seem the least bit flustered by everything on her plate. I was truly amazed by Mrs. Menulli.

"You're just a regular *Superwoman*, aren't you?" I remarked after obtaining her medical history.

"I guess you could say that," she replied with a smile. The nickname stuck.

I saw Superwoman once a month at the beginning of her pregnancy, then every two weeks at the start of the third trimester. She continued to manage the responsibilities of home and work with seemingly little difficulty. I usually began our visit with the words, "Hello, Superwoman. How are you doing today?"

Her pregnancy continued uneventfully until thirty-two

weeks. She mentioned in passing that she had episodes when her heart would race. These lasted a short period of time. I was a little bit surprised. This was Superwoman after all.

"Do you have a history of heart problems?" I asked.

"No, never," she responded. Her heart exam was normal.

"Do you drink a lot of caffeine?" I inquired.

"I have been drinking quite a bit of coffee lately," she admitted.

"It would be a good idea to cut back," I informed her. "All that caffeine may be contributing to your symptoms. Let's cut back your caffeine to one cup a day and see how you are doing at your next visit." She agreed with a smile.

I saw Mrs. Manulli in my office two weeks later for her regular visit. She had drastically decreased her caffeine intake and her heart was no longer racing. Things were back to normal.

At thirty-six weeks, her husband accompanied her to the next appointment—his first. I asked Mrs. Manulli how she was doing. There was a brief pause on her part. Then she said, "My heart has been racing again, even more than before."

"How is your caffeine intake?" I inquired. She paused again.

"I have been drinking a little bit more coffee lately," came the reluctant reply. Mr. Manulli was listening intently. He spoke up for his wife.

"She drinks coffee *all the time,* doc! I have been telling her she needs to cut back."

Mrs. Manulli looked straight at me with calm disapproval as I fidgeted uncomfortably in my seat. Apparently, I had opened a big can of worms. Superwoman's caffeine habit was exposed, and she was being reprimanded publicly for it by her spouse. By the way Mrs. Manulli looked at me, I could tell she held me responsible for this personal affront.

Mr. Manulli looked at his watch and stood to his feet. "Ah!

It's a quarter to four doc,. I have to go to work." He gave his wife a pat on the shoulder and walked out of my office to go to his job. I watched with dread as Mr. Manulli walked out of my office, leaving me alone with his chastised wife. I will never forget the growing smile on Mrs. Manulli's face as her husband left the room.

I felt like a small mouse trapped in a corner by a very big cat—a cat amused by my predicament and discomfort, biding her time to pounce on me at any moment. Her silence was unnerving. I had to get out of this predicament as quickly as possible.

"Well, Mrs. Manulli, I guess that will do it for today. We will need to see you back in a week." I remained seated behind my desk for safety.

"Very well," she said, staring at me for the last time. She got up from her chair, turned around, and slowly started walking toward the hallway that led out of my office. Mrs. Manulli didn't say a word about the coffee incident. Did this mean she was going to let me off the hook for bringing it up? I had to know.

"Are we still friends?" I asked reluctantly as she approached the door. Superwoman did not turn around or slow her pace. "I'll think about it," she replied matter-of-factly, before disappearing down the hallway.

I breathed a huge sigh of relief, sat back in my leather chair, and contemplated the incident. I learned a valuable lesson that day. You don't tug on Superman's cape.[1] You don't talk about Superwoman's caffeine.

[1] Lyrics from the song *You Don't Mess Around With Jim*, by Jim Croce.

The Seed of Hope

Ulaanbatar, in north-central Mongolia, is the coldest capital city in the world. Each year for just a short while, it comes out of hibernation. During the month of August the central plaza is teeming with people—buying, selling, just trying to survive.

Four American doctors were outside the market building planning the next item on their itinerary for the day. They were part of a medical team partnering with the Mongolian government on a humanitarian mission. Now it was time to head back to the States, and the group was enjoying a day of shopping and sightseeing.

Even though it was leisure time, Dr. Thornton, one of the Americans, couldn't help but notice a boy who looked to be about ten years old eating an ice cream cone. The boy was dirty and wore only filthy rags. He was more than likely homeless.

Suddenly, some of the older street kids ran up to him and stole his ice cream cone! There was nothing the child could do. They were bigger and stronger. The little boy, who was used to a hard life, sat down in the street and began to cry, wiping the tears from his face with his dirty hands.

Dr. Thornton could not stop looking at the boy. He recognized hopelessness when he saw it. He had experienced it himself before he met Jesus. To see no hope on the face of someone so young was more than he could bear.

The surgeon excused himself from his colleagues and walked up to the boy. He motioned for the boy to follow him into the market building, and the boy complied. Dr. Thornton led the boy into a meat store, where he motioned for him to sit at a small plastic table. There in the restaurant he was safe from the street kids who had been harassing him. Once the boy was seated, the doctor ordered one-fourth of a rotisserie chicken and gave it to the child.

The hungry child looked into the foreigner's face with amazement and was surprised to see that the man had a large, red birthmark under his right eye. He stared for just a moment before taking the chicken and beginning to feast on it. Dr. Thornton smiled and returned to his friends.

"What happened?" Wendy, the dermatologist, asked.

"He was hungry," Dr. Thornton answered. "I bought him something to eat."

"That was a real nice thing to do, Nick," said Wendy.

"He'll be hungry again in no time, but the poor kid looked like he had lost all hope. Maybe a simple kindness will help him keep going when the hard times come again. None of us could survive without hope," replied Dr. Thornton.

Over the years, Dr. Thornton wondered what ever happened to that little boy. On that one day, at least, he had helped a little and planted a seed of hope.

* * * * * * *

Batukhan looked out the large window at the capital city. Much had changed in thirty years. He thought about that day at the street market many years ago. He was a homeless beggar boy back then. His father had died before he was born. His single mother could not make enough to feed all her children.

One day, she dropped him off at the market plaza. He was just six years old.

The boy made the best of it, surviving on scraps and begging for food. The market was his home. The winters were very cold, and very lonely. But the memory of a foreigner's kindness kept him going. He was ten that summer. Some bullies had stolen an ice cream cone a vendor had given him. He remembered his anger, hating his life, hating people, and being ready to give up altogether. And he remembered the painted man.

The foreigner had pointed to a meat market and gestured for him to follow. Inside, the man had seated him at a plastic table and purchased a big piece of chicken just for him. He remembered looking up and smiling at the man, who had a big, red birthmark under his right eye. Then he focused all his attention on the meal, eating it all so the bullies could not take it from him. When he looked up again, the man was gone.

That chicken dinner was the only meal Batukhan would eat for the next two days. He was becoming desperate again. Then he suddenly had an idea. Maybe there were other foreigners like the painted man who would help him. He had heard about some foreign women who had a home for orphans. They wore strange black dresses with black-and-white headpieces. He later found out they were called nuns. They dressed differently but they were very nice to him. He washed his face with water to clean himself before going to talk to them.

When he arrived at the orphanage, he pleaded with the older nun and the young nun to take him in. He promised to behave and work hard if they would just give him a place to live. Sisters Rosemary and Josephine could not say no. They escorted him into the orphanage, one on each side, an arm over his back. Batukhan at age twelve now had a real home.

Batukhan thrived at the orphanage under the nuns' care. He learned to read and write, and he learned about Jesus and God. He helped care for and teach the younger orphans. At age seventeen, he attended the local university. He graduated in three years and became a military officer. After an illustrious twenty-year career, he became a general at age forty. General Batukhan, was very popular with the people. He retired from military service and was elected president the following year.

The homeless boy who had become president now gazed at Ulaanbatar from the window of the National Palace, as he remembered that day in the central market. Soon, though, his thoughts were interrupted by a knock on the door.

"Excuse me, Mr. President," his aide said. "A foreigner has requested an audience with you. The man says he has been coming to Mongolia for many years providing help for the people. He is asking for a sizeable amount of land for a project. The man spoke first with the mayor, who has sent him to make his petition to you."

"Please bring him in," said the president. His aide left the room and closed the door behind him. When he returned, there was a tall, lean, pleasant man in his sixties at his side. The man's gray hair was combed back neatly. He was wearing a comfortable three-piece black suit, black shirt, and green tie. He had thin-rimmed glasses and a warm smile. Under his right eye, there was a three-inch red birthmark. He might have been thirty years older, but Batukhan recognized him at once.

"It is an honor to meet you, Mr. President," said Dr. Nick Thornton, giving him a warm, sincere handshake. Batukhan responded in kind.

"It is an honor for me as well," he replied. "What can I do for you?"

"Well, sir, I fell in love with your country many years ago. I have been coming here ever since, providing medical teams to help care for the people at no charge. I am asking for land to start a ranch for orphan boys. It is my hope to provide them with a loving home and an education at no expense to your government."

"Does this ranch have a name, Doctor?" Batukhan asked.

"Yes, Mr. President. The ranch will be called the Seed of Hope." Batukhan rolled the words around in his mind, remembering the seed of hope this man had given him three decades earlier.

"I will gladly give you land for your ranch," he answered without hesitation.

Dr. Thornton was both surprised and delighted by the president's quick response.

"Thank you, Mr. President! You have no idea how much I appreciate this. I promise you, this ranch will be a big help to the Mongolian people," Dr. Thornton said.

"You have already helped the Mongolian people more than you know, Doctor," he said softly, his eyes watering. He placed his arm around Dr. Thornton's shoulder, escorting him to the door. "Please, allow me to buy you lunch," he said, as they were about to leave his office.

"Thank you, Mr. President! That is very kind of you," he replied.

"I would like to share a story with you," he told Nick with a warm smile, donning his coat and hat as the two friends went out for a bite to eat."

The Sign on the Door

You know it's time to make home improvements when your seventeen-year-old spends her entire $450 in savings to fix up the master bedroom while you're out of town for a few days. While I was on-call delivering babies and performing surgery, she was busy moving furniture, painting walls, and hanging curtains, candle sconces, and wall art. This was no small task for one person. When I returned and found out about Rebekah's project, I helped with a recliner, artificial plants, accent tables, and lamps.

My wife, Libby, was in Kentucky when these improvements were made. She came home to a real surprise. She was speechless for several minutes, taking in the transformation a little at a time.

I regret to say our bedroom used to look more like a bad second office than a romantic master. My teenage daughter's loving idea to update our bedroom made me realize that we could make other improvements that would make our home environment more livable. My life changed when she introduced me to HGTV.

I'm not ashamed to say that HGTV changed my life. Go ahead and laugh, it's okay. I can take it. You don't understand, however, how far I've come. The heart knows its own bitterness, and a stranger does not share its joy.[1] Before HGTV this physician and surgeon didn't have a clue about interior design.

My perspective grew when I learned terms like color palette, texture, focal point, scale to size, and functionality, just to name a few. I excitedly shared what I learned on HGTV with the nurses and staff at the hospital. We compared notes, and I discovered a large network of home improvement amateurs who were as excited about interior design as I was. Wow!

After several weeks of watching home improvement shows, I was ready to put what I learned into practice. I painted the laundry room as well as the hallway between the library and den. I installed new chandeliers in the entry hallway and dining room, as well as pendant lighting in the kitchen. I replaced the front door handle and porch light with more elegant ones. I painted Rebekah's room—after all, she had painted my room. The family also painted our middle daughter, Victoria's room.

At that point, I was feeling pretty good about my home improvement skills. I started looking around the house for my next project. That's when I decided to take on the downstairs guest bathroom.

No upgrades (another word I learned) had been made to the guest bathroom since the house was built fifteen years ago. The green wallpaper was nice but dated. You could almost hear the walls saying, "Makeover please!" The space contained your basic white ceramic toilet and pedestal sink with manufacturer's gold-trimmed mirror, light fixture, faucet, towel holder, paper dispenser, door knobs, and hinges. We added a Victorian marble-top wash stand and floral picture frames to the small room. Wood laminate flooring finished off the space. Remember the laminate flooring, that's important. After a decade and a half of status quo, I decided to give the guest bathroom a much-needed face lift.

The project got off to a good start. I visited the home

improvement store (HIS for short) down the street and purchased the necessary primer and paint. Rebekah, our seventeen-year-old artist, picked out a rich creamy chocolate brown paint for the walls and ceiling. I replaced the rectangular gold-trimmed mirror with an oval-shaped contemporary one. The gold light fixture was removed and an oiled, bronze fixture accented by two elegant sandy porcelain globes was hung in its place. The gold towel holder was replaced by a sophisticated oiled bronze one. The old toilet paper dispenser imbedded in the wall was switched to a white ceramic one instead. I custom ordered heavy oiled bronze triple-switch and electric-outlet plate covers to match. My big splurge was a Victorian single-handle, oiled bronze faucet that would replace the current gold water faucet knobs. I would pay a plumber to install the new faucet. I also replaced the gold door knobs and hinges with, you guessed it, oiled bronze ones. I added several floating mantels on the walls for candles and artwork—to scale of course.

As I surveyed the new and improved guest bathroom after several days of hard work and multiple trips to stores, I was quite pleased with myself. I eventually wanted to replace the white ceramic toilet and pedestal sink with soft creamy ones, but the originals would do for now. Then something caught my eye as I took in every square inch of the newly renovated space. It was the gold toilet bowl handle. It stood out like a sore thumb now that every metal thing in the bathroom was oiled bronze.

I stared at the little gold toilet bowl handle for several minutes not knowing what to do. I then came up with a great idea, or so I thought. "Surely they make oiled bronze toilet bowl handles," I thought to myself. "I'll just pick one up at the store and replace the handle we have now. *How hard can it be?*"

Ladies, listen carefully. Maybe some of you have already learned this the hard way. When your husband is doing a home-improvement project and he utters the words *how hard can it be*, what that really means is *trouble*!

How hard can it be is synonymous with

1) a red flag;
2) the sound of ice cracking under your feet;
3) a warning sign saying that the bridge is out;
4) the flashing lights at a train crossing;
5) dark clouds before a storm.

This is what *how hard can it be* really means: "I don't know what I'm doing and I am gullible enough to believe it is all going to work out—somehow. I am not going to ask for help because I have convinced myself I can figure it out on my own without repercussions. I can do this even though I really don't have a clue. Surely I can't get into that much trouble if I mess up." Uh-huh, yeah right. The fallacy in this reasoning is that disaster is somehow fortuitously avoidable, when in actuality it is fundamentally inevitable. What follows is an account of what happened to me after I uttered those famous last words.

The very next day, I purchased an oiled bronze toilet bowl handle for fifteen dollars and returned home excited about putting the final touch on the guest bathroom. My cell phone rang as I was about to get started. Libby called to let me know she would be home in thirty minutes. *I'll be finished before she gets here*, I thought.

I walked into the bathroom with the replacement handle, pulled it out of the box, and surveyed the piece for a moment. *It will look great on the toilet bowel,* I thought to myself. I looked at the instructions on the back of the box and learned that there were only about four steps. *This will be easy,* I remember thinking.

I read step number one: remove old toilet handle. I took the toilet lid off the bowl and examined the old handle resting above the water line. *Piece of cake,* I thought. I was so confident the task would go smoothly that I didn't bother emptying the toilet bowel or closing the shut-off valve. Yes, I have written a book on decision-making.

I applied my wrench to the nut on the inside of the toilet bowl handle and started trying to turn the thing. It didn't budge. I tried a little harder and still nothing happened. By this time I was getting a little frustrated, being so close to the finish line. I later found out you turn the wrench in the *opposite* direction in order to loosen the nut on toilet bowl handles! Everyone at work seemed to know this but me. So instead of *loosening* the nut on the toilet handle, I was actually *tightening* it.

In a moment of mounting frustration and carelessness, I cranked on the wrench with too much force. Suddenly, the entire left side of the ceramic toilet bowl broke off, and three gallons of water poured out like a busted miniature dam. I let out an audible gasp as the bathroom floor flooded with an inch of water and the water spout in the toilet bowl went off like a geyser. The broken chunk of ceramic in my left hand was still connected to the rubber lid in the bowl by the chain on the handle. I frantically reached down to turn off the shut-off valve, set the side of the tank down, and raced to the laundry room for towels. Brownie, my labradoodle, sat about six feet from the bathroom watching the commotion. I could almost hear her thinking, *You goofed.* Once the flood had subsided, I surveyed the damage. The toilet was demolished. The laminate floor was soaked. The warped floor around the base of the toilet would be even more noticeable now. *How could I have been so careless?* I thought. The truth was—I knew. It was pride. Pride goes before destruction, and a haughty spirit before a fall.[2]

My mind was racing. Libby would be home in about ten minutes. How was I going to explain this to her? The toilet would need to be replaced right away. I wanted a new cream-colored toilet. The white pedestal sink would have to be replaced with a cream-colored one to match as well. Oh well.

The old me would have been angry after a mishap like this—angry at myself, angry at the toilet, and angry at the toilet manufacturer, even though it was all my fault. I was teaching a class at church on Wednesday nights on the fruit of the Spirit at the time.[3] *I am not going to lose my peace. I am not going to lose my joy,* I told myself. Right there I decided to turn this blunder into something the whole family could laugh about.

I calmly walked over to my desk in the library and pulled a page of college-ruled paper out of the drawer. I wrote the words OUT OF ORDER in big capital letters, taped the sheet to the door, and closed it behind me. I exited the house, got in the car, and drove to the HIS in search of a new cream-colored toilet.

I had been looking at toilets and sinks for ten minutes, when my cell phone rang as expected. I knew it was Libby, and I knew what she was going to say. "Honey—what happened to the toilet in the bathroom?"

My ego shrunk another size as I proceeded to explain to her what had occurred. I told her where I was and that I was looking for a replacement toilet and sink.

"Can I join you?" she asked.

"Sure," I said, relieved she wasn't upset about the mishap. She wanted to help find a new toilet and sink.

We looked around the store for several more minutes and couldn't decide what to buy. Libby and I decided to go to another HIS and look there as well. They had a bigger selection on display. After looking at all the display samples and catalogues, Libby chose a custom-made, modern black toilet and pedestal sink. The warped laminate flooring in the bathroom, and outside hallway, had to be replaced with tile that matched that in the den. *Ka-ching.*

I must admit, when it was all finished it looked great. That is how one last fifteen-dollar upgrade turned into a three-thousand-dollar upgrade. *How hard can it be?*

The sign on the door brought one more laugh. Our daughter Victoria was taking a nap upstairs while I was trying to contain the flood in the bathroom. She came downstairs while Libby and I were at the HIS. Still half-asleep, she read the sign on the door somewhat confused. "OUT OF ORDER? *How can the whole bathroom be out of order?*" she asked herself. She opened the door, looked at the devastation, and what do you think she said next? "Dad did this!"

[1] Proverbs 14:10

[2] Proverbs 16:18

[3] Galatians 5:22–23

The Two Coins

It was that time of year again in the empire of Kambola. The Festival of Gifts had arrived. During this celebration, people exchanged gifts as a tribute to the nation's peace and prosperity. The Festival of Gifts was always enjoyable, but the highlight of the celebration was the King's Gift Ceremony. During this public ceremony, people would present a gift of great value to the king, who would then judge the gifts and declare a winner to be honored in a manner of the king's choosing. This was the protocol of the land.

That night the great hall of the king was crowded with people excited to see what special gifts would be presented this year. When the sound of trumpets announced to all that the King's Gift Ceremony had begun, everyone became instantly silent. The king, with his majestic robe and crown, sat high on his throne while all below remained standing. In his right hand he held the royal scepter, the symbol of his power.

The silence was broken when the King's chief counselor sang out, "Does anyone have a gift of great value for the king?"

Protocol required that those who wished to present a gift come forward one at a time, state their name, and place their gift before the throne. The first person to step forward was a wealthy merchant. He stated his name and presented the king with the title to a large piece of forest land with a newly built house for the king's leisure hunting. The crowd roared their approval as the merchant set the deed on the wooden table before the steps to the throne.

After a brief pause, a lady stepped forward. She stated her name and presented the king with a blanket made of the finest materials, containing threads of silver and gold. The blanket had images of the empire's glorious history and culture. She had spent a year preparing her gift for the king. The audience shouted and applauded as she set her gift on the wooden table before the throne.

Shortly thereafter, another man stepped forward leading a magnificent white horse by the reins. The horse—never having been defeated in a long-distance race—was well known throughout the empire. The man presented the horse as a gift to the king's stables. Once again, the audience roared in approval.

The atmosphere was electrifying. Each gift seemed greater than the one before. The audience applauded longer with each presentation.

The next person presented the king with a beautiful instrumental song, composed in the king's honor. Another brought a new scientific discovery that would benefit everyone in the kingdom.

All of these gifts met with approval from the people as well as a smile and nod of acceptance by the king. After nine people had stated their names and come forward with their gifts, the chief counselor proclaimed, "Is there anyone left with a gift of great value for the king?"

A moment of silence passed, and then someone stepped out of the crowd into the open. It was a certain poor widow whose face was concealed by a hood. She walked slowly to the table before the great throne, grasping something small and unseen in her right hand. The crowd murmured, some in disbelief, others with indignation. Didn't she know that insulting the king could have serious consequences?

The king gazed intently at the poor widow as she approached. She stopped in front of the table on which all the splendid gifts had been placed. She then bowed to the ground before the king and said, "My name is Nanna. I wish to give you all my livelihood, sire." With that, she laid two copper coins on the table.[1]

Outraged, the captain of the guard stepped forward and lifted the woman to her feet and pulled back the hood that covered her face. He allowed the king time to see the woman before him before turning her around to face the audience. A collective gasp went up as they saw the woman's scarred and disfigured face. The captain then reached for his axe and shouted, "For this you will surely die!"

But before he could swing the axe, the King shouted for him to stop! Silence fell on the great hall as the captain lowered his axe.

"Is—is that you, Nanna?" the king whispered. He had not spoken those words in thirty years. "I am here, sire," came the reply.

The king had been an eight-year-old boy the last time he heard that beautiful, soft voice say "I am here, sire." From the moment of his birth, everything the young prince needed had been taken care of by a young maiden devoted to the queen, his mother. The young maiden fed and cared for him, played games with him, read him stories. Often they walked together in the gardens. The first word spoken by the young prince was "Nanna." Each time he heard her soft steps coming his way, he would call out, "Is that you, Nanna?" The reply was always the same. A sweet, delicate voice would say, "I am here, sire."

One day, the prince and his beloved Nanna were playing

in the royal gardens, when a wild dog managed to enter the royal grounds. Unaware of the danger, the boy looked up only in time to see the crazed animal racing toward him—and then Nanna stepping between them. The animal viciously attacked the defenseless maiden, pulling her to the ground and tearing into the flesh on her face and body. Her life was spared only because the royal guards came to her rescue.

The last time the young prince saw Nanna she was lying motionless on the ground, blood covering her face and arms. The boy tried to run to her, but one of the guards stopped him. He was led back to the palace and never saw Nanna again—until that moment as she stood before his throne.

Suddenly the king did the unthinkable. He jumped up from his throne and raced down the steps to where the old widow stood. He threw his arms around her and hugged her with great tenderness.

"All these years," the king said, "all these years, I thought that you were dead. But here you are."

"I could not stand the thought of you seeing me this way, sire, and so I left the royal service. I married an honorable man and we lived in peace and quiet far away in the country. When my husband died, I was impoverished. I had to move back to the city in order to survive. I hope you will forgive me this intrusion, Sire. Even though I knew it might cost me my life, I wanted to experience the joy of seeing your face one more time."

The king took off his necklace with the royal seal and placed it around the widow's neck. "You have given me the gift of greatest value, Nanna. You have given me your heart. From this day forward you will eat at my table."

[1] Luke 21:1–4

The Spaghetti Mama

They say a little sugar goes a long way. It took me six weeks in the summer of 1987 to figure that out. Libby and I were newlyweds for two weeks before I was shipped off to beautiful Fort Riley, Kansas, for a month-and-a-half-long ROTC cadet advanced camp for future men and women army officers. That is the technical term for it. Would you like to know what that means in plain English? It means having your head shaved, living in barracks with thirty guys, getting up at five o'clock every morning to do PT, eating in the chow hall three times a day, and working until ten o'clock at night when you hear the words *lights out*! Get the picture?

Needless to say, I wanted to be back home with my little woman. We were newlyweds after all. I kept a picture of my new bride with me wherever I went. But I have to say that the discipline, military training, physical fitness, camaraderie, and character-building experiences at Fort Riley helped to toughen me up and make a better man out of me. Those memories will be etched in my mind forever.

Fort Riley was the long-time home of the Big Red One, an infantry division. During my time there I experienced survival training, land navigation, rifle range practice, and grenade throwing. I also learned what to do when a tornado warning siren goes off in the middle of the night. We were in Kansas after all.

One of my best memories is the time our squad, one of the sixteen squads in the company, won the physical fitness obstacle course competition. Our ragtag group didn't look like much on the outside, but that didn't matter to us. We called ourselves the black sheep and we were champs!

Even the obstacle course glory, however, was not my most memorable experience at beautiful Fort Riley. That took place in the Chow Hall, where I met the Spaghetti Mama.

She was a large woman. At five feet, nine inches tall, she had a big body, big legs, big arms, a big neck, and big hair. Even her voice was big. She was, to say the least, an imposing figure. We walked into the army version of Luby's Cafeteria wearing our camouflage uniforms with our trays, plates, and silverware. We then handed our plates to one of two female civilian servers, who gave us one scoop of whatever was in the food container in front of them. The Spaghetti Mama was one of these two servers.

Everyone got the same amount of food regardless of whether they were male or female, short or tall, large or small. There were no seconds, and we knew better than to ask for more. If someone failed to pay attention and was moving too slowly, we heard "next!" and that was that!

Spaghetti Mama's coworker was a shorter version and just as intimidating. I *never* saw a cadet ask for more food from either one of them. Those girls could whack you on the head and knock you out with their serving spoons, and we were sure they would do just that if we so much as requested more mashed potatoes. It was those modest portions that helped me get lean and fit.

Six weeks at advanced camp finally passed and I was going back home to my beautiful bride, who was waiting patiently for me in Texas. We were all excited about returning to our loved ones and our normal daily lives. I still remember my last meal in the chow hall before getting on the bus that would take us to the airport and eventually back to the real world.

When our turn came in the chow line, the two sisters were waiting for us, performing their duties as usual. I saw the huge food bins with pasta and meat sauce in front of them. Something inside of me rose up the moment I saw that spaghetti. I don't know if it was my love for Italian food, the fact that I was tired of leaving the chow hall hungry, or the fact that I was on my way home. For whatever reason, I was feeling a bit cocky.

"Give me something I can remember you by," I said to her, handing her my plate. The transformation was astounding! Her demeanor changed completely. She went from a plain, routine expression to an excited and friendly one.

"Oh, baby!" she said, as she poured one scoopful of pasta and meat sauce after the other on my plate. You would have thought I had proposed to the girl. The Lord is my witness I meant nothing romantic or provocative by my request. I was a married man. All I wanted was a decent serving of spaghetti. When she couldn't heap one more noodle onto my plate, she handed it over with a smile. I sat down and ate until I could eat no more!

I learned many things during my time at Fort Riley, Kansas. My thoughts always end up drifting to the mess hall, though. I still think about my conversation with that lady in the chow line. It taught me some valuable lessons. People aren't always what they seem. Thank you for teaching me that Spaghetti Mama. I will never forget you.

The Stir-Fry

After more than a quarter century of iron-clad secrecy, my wife, Libby, has given me permission to de-classify the family file known as The Stir-Fry. To be perfectly honest with you, I never thought this day would come. After twenty-five years of marriage, I can count on one hand the number of times I have been allowed to share this tale over dinner with our closest friends. The result is the same every time: breath-catching, tear-releasing laughter.

A little embarrassing for Mrs. Tillotson, perhaps, but it is a great yarn about love's perseverance. I believe Libby's stance on sharing The Stir-Fry has softened over the years by observing how much enjoyment people derive from hearing the tale. I asked her one day if she wouldn't mind me writing The Stir-Fry story, thinking it was a long shot at best. To my surprise, she agreed! I am publishing this as quickly as possible before she changes her mind.

It was the spring of 1985 in East Texas, where we were attending college. The weather was perfect, the birds were chirping, the flowers were blooming, and boy squirrels were chasing the girl squirrels. In a nutshell, love was in the air.

Libby and I had been dating for only a week. She invited me over to her apartment for lunch.

"Can I fix you some stir-fry?" she asked.

"Sure," I said, thinking she must be pretty good at

preparing this kind of food. Why else would she ask? To be honest, stir-fry is not really one of my favorite entrees, but I enjoy some every once in a while. I later discovered Libby likes to try new things in the kitchen and doesn't always follow the instructions in the cookbook. It can be a blessing, but on some occasions there is a price to pay. Can you say *hard lesson*?

I sat at the kitchen table while Libby placed the vegetables in a wok. I wasn't paying close attention as she poured too much oil in the mix. I was enjoying our conversation too much to notice her cooking. We sat together at the table and ate what appeared to be a wholesome meal. It didn't take long for the exotic vegetables and excess grease to do a number on me. I was curled up in a ball on the couch in no time.

You may be thinking, "He has a weak stomach. That's why he got sick." Let me explain something to you. I grew up in Guatemala. I have eaten turtles and iguanas. I can eat just about *anything* served on my plate as long as it is not alive and doesn't bite me back. The one thing I don't handle well, however, is greasy food. In this case, it was greasy stir-fry.

They say the way to a man's heart is through his stomach. I had an epiphany in that moment. The way to a man's *grave* is through his stomach as well! Libby was really concerned about me, and rightfully so. I wasn't looking too good, and in her mind this didn't bode well for our fledgling relationship. As she watched me groan in agony, she thought the *relationship* was over. I thought my *life* was over!

I survived that initial stir-fry ordeal, as you have surmised. Contrary to Libby's initial concerns at the time, the relationship was not over. We married and at the time of this writing are on the verge of celebrating our silver anniversary. I didn't marry Libby for her cooking. I married Libby because I love her.

We rarely eat stir-fry in our home. Libby never offers to

cook any, and I don't ask her to make it for me. It's sort of an unwritten rule in our house. Until recently, I rarely joked about the stir-fry with Libby. She didn't find the tale quite as humorous as I did.

I couldn't comprehend for years why Libby didn't like being reminded about the stir-fry. I thought, "Hey, I'm the one who almost died! If I can laugh about it, surely she can." I slowly realized she thought I was being critical of her cooking, which I wasn't. Let me set the record straight. My wife is an excellent cook. She makes the best beef stroganoff in the world! Her chili and spaghetti are amazing as well. The list goes on and on. She's gained a great deal of valuable experience over the years…at my expense.

Libby often asks me what I want to have for dinner. I ponder the question in my mind, and occasionally my thoughts drift back to stir-fry in 1985. *What do you want for dinner?* I have come to realize how powerful those words really are. *Stroganoff* or *stir-fry,*I ask myself silently. Hmmh.

"I would love stroganoff tonight, honey," I respond with the most innocent smile I can conjure up.

The Watchman

Carl stood at his station while the inmates ate dinner. His gray uniform and badge identified him as a member of the Department of Corrections (DOC). He was an easygoing man who took his job seriously.

Carl had moved his family just six months ago. Back in Colorado he had worked as a prison guard as well. He and Lisa and their two small girls were finally getting settled in. Lisa worked at a local bank while the girls were making friends at their new school. Carl's transfer from one medium security unit to another was proving to be a smooth one.

The other guards had told him the food was good in this unit, and so far they had been right. They gave the credit to the chef, a popular guy who had been around for a long time.

On this particular day, Carl was assigned to the lunch room. He surveyed the room as the last shift of inmates were finishing up. He watched as the inmates got up from their tables and headed to their cells for the "count," part of the daily routine. Carl knew from experience how important routine is in a place like this.

As they passed Carl on their way out of the lunchroom, one of the inmates named Rick paused to say hello. The man, also known as the "Watchman," always had a smile on his face. Carl figured it was because he had only two months and eleven days left to serve. On the outside, Rick had a successful auto parts business and a supportive family. After serving almost three years for illegal business practices, he swore he'd learned his lesson—and realigned his priorities. God, family, and others, that's what it's all about. He could hardly wait to get back to his life and all the little things he missed—eating out, watching movies with the family, church on Sundays.

Carl returned Rick's greeting and then watched him head down the hall toward the cell block. The count went off without a hitch, always a good thing.

* * * * * * * * *

After the count, Rick settled into his usual routine. He had been without a cellmate since Hank the Tank, had gone home two weeks earlier. Rick smiled at the thought of Hank reuniting with his wife and kids. "I can't wait to get home and hug my wife and kids," he would tell Rick every single day. "God, family, and others, Rick, that's what it's all about."

Rick chuckled to himself at the memory. "I'm right there with you, buddy. It'll be my turn soon!" Hank had been Rick's only cell mate during his stay at Harrington Prison, also known as "Dogwood" because of all the dogwood trees outside the perimeter. The men had become close after Hank had led Rick back to the Lord.

After the evening count, inmates typically disperse in all directions. Some go to classes. Most congregate downstairs to play games and watch television. Rick's cell was on the second floor, in a corner, out of the way, and on that night as he did every night, he decided to stay put. He had just gotten comfortable on the bottom bunk when he heard a familiar voice. *Hello, Rick, how are you doing?* It was Jesus.

"I am doing well, Lord. Where are we going tonight?"

Rick's work shift was about to start. He was a watchman for the kingdom of heaven.

Tonight we are going to India. My people are suffering terrible persecution there. I need someone to stand in the gap for that part of My Body.

"Okay, Lord," came the reply. Rick got on his knees, as he and other watchmen around the world began praying. Dark clouds in the heavens rolled in over India. There was the mighty roar of thunder and crackling of lightning as the Holy Spirit rained down over southern Asia. All the while, Rick and his fellow watchmen around the world prayed.[1]

[1] Isaiah 62:6

I hope you have enjoyed reading Volume 1 of *The Chicken Bus Girl Stories* as much as I enjoyed writing them. Other stories to look for in Volume 2 include "The Committee," "The Windows of Heaven Store," "The Return of The Chicken Bus Girl," and more. Until next time!

For His glory,
Nathan Tillotson

Nathan Tillotson is an OB/GYN physician and surgeon, former military officer, and international speaker. God has gifted him with the ability to simplify and teach biblical principles in a way that is methodical and easy to understand, using great stories and illustrations. Dr. Nathan's desire is to give people practical, biblical strategies for victorious living. He and his wife, Libby, have three daughters, Katherine, Victoria, and Rebekah.

JUJIPUBLISHING.COM

Teaching * Training * Transforming
To Contact Author
Visit our Web Site: Jujipublishing.com